Loving Lindsey

An American Dream Love Story

Book Two

by

Josephine Parker

Editing by Chameleon
Graphics Design by S.G. Hawkins

For Teri

Acknowledgment

Theodore Roosevelt once said, *"The credit belongs to the man who is actually in the arena, whose face is marred by dust, and sweat, and blood; who strives valiantly; who errs, who comes short again and again, because there is no effort without error and shortcoming; but who does actually strive to do the deeds; who knows great enthusiasms, the great devotions; who spends himself in a worthy cause; who at the best, knows in the end the triumph of high achievement, and who, at the worst, if he fails, at least fails while daring greatly."*

I scooted into the arena with a healthy nudge from an amazing group of friends, family, and beta readers, all of whom supported me along the way. My parents told me I could do anything and be anyone. My sister believed in my talent. My friends were there to listen when I cried, and cheer when I smiled. They all said, "Keep going." A greater fortune I could not imagine.

In particular, I'd like to thank Marilynn, Milt, Teri, Laurie H., Beth B., Melissa W., and Lauri O. You are the people most special to me in this world. Thank you for believing in me.

I would also like to thank Chameleon for her excellent editing, her guidance, and sharing her wealth of information. And S.G. Hawkins Graphic Design for tirelessly working to create the covers I envisioned.

Table of Contents

Chapter 1: Lindsey

Lindsey jerked to a stop as the metal arm came down in front of her bumper. She clenched the steering wheel in both hands as her eyes darted around, seeing for the first time a sign that read, "Restricted Access. Faculty Only."

No, no, no, she muttered to herself, looking at the clock. She couldn't be late. Her invitation already felt like a joke. Her body went suddenly cold as she considered the possibility her offer could be rescinded.

There was a stretch of black asphalt just beyond the arm, beckoning her to pull forward and pick one of the few empty spots just ahead. From the corner of her eye, she saw a thick man emerge from a tiny, white guard station and stroll toward her driver's side window. He stood beside her door and mouthed something she couldn't hear. He exhaled visibly and made a twirling motion with his hand, instructing her to roll down the window.

As she did, her chest tightened.

"I'll ask again," the guard said, "you faculty?"

Lindsey blinked in response, her hand darting out instinctively to grope at the worn cover of her tablet. She had mapped out her route, even looked at a satellite image. This road was supposed to go through to public parking, not faculty parking only. She swallowed and wished silently, once again, that reality matched the virtual world. She should have dug further. Tomorrow, she would hack into the software and update the mapping data. While she was at it, she should hack this school. Why did they accept her anyway? No, scratch that. Google "fear of success." That was a better plan.

"Miss," the guard said, snapping her back to the gentle idling of her car, and the red and white striped bar that blocked her path forward. "There's another car pulling up behind you. What's it gonna be?"

"Um," Lindsey stammered, dipping her head forward to peer up at the ancient stone bell-tower that loomed just a block away. "The President's Pavilion is right there. I see it. I—"

"True, but you can't get there from here...unless you're faculty."

You can't get there from here. Story of my life, Lindsey thought, her arms tensing. As she did, she felt a tiny prick against her skin. She mentally shook her head, remembering that she hadn't removed the price tag from her dress. *Way to go, Lindsey. Be late and show up with a tag sticking out of your dress.* If she had just worn something old she would've had time to find another lot. Her new apartment was stacked high with boxes filled with outfits, but she hadn't even opened them, she didn't know where anything went here.

Lindsey's eyes darted to her rear view mirror, where another car waited. She gave the driver a little wave before turning back toward the guard. "Listen," she said quickly, forcing a smile. "I'm late. Wait, please, don't shake your head. Today is a big deal...at least for me. Couldn't you make an exception and let me through, just for an hour?"

"Nope. Gotta turn around," he said before walking back into his guard station and plopping down into the single worn chair that waited inside. As he sat, he glanced back at Lindsey's face. She must have looked miserable because his eyebrows unpinned from between his eyes and dropped softly, revealing rows of laugh lines embedded in his skin. With some effort, he stood back up and walked gingerly toward her window. "Miss," he said, leaning in, "I am not unsympathetic. Truly. But this road, and all of the parking beyond it, is for faculty only. Don't know if you're aware, but parking is at a premium in downtown Boston. The university gobbled up all these lots last year, part for new construction, part for more faculty. People take their parking pretty serious here." He leaned back and made a show of inspecting her windshield before leaning back in. "However, even though I don't see a decal, sometimes new faculty don't get it right away. So, I'll ask you again," he said conspiratorially, "you faculty?"

Lindsey twisted her lips to the side in an effort to stop a nervous laugh from escaping. It had been ten years since she had stepped foot on a college campus, and she thought maybe by now she *could* pass for faculty. She looked again at the road ahead and considered telling a small fib, but...she was a terrible liar. "No," she admitted.

"That's too bad, I guess," the guard said with a thoughtful smile.

Lindsey sighed, thinking back to this morning. As she followed her moving truck down the highway, the familiar streets of Worcester gave way to the skyscrapers and narrow streets of historic Boston. Every building seemed to crowd its way on top of another building. After an hour, she and the truck finally crammed awkwardly into an empty space and the movers began unloading.

Lindsey sat idly on the front stoop as they heaved her boxes onto their backs and packed them up the narrow staircase of her new building, cursing and waving through the neighborhood residents who honked and veered around the truck's rumbling front-end.

As they worked, Lindsey daydreamed about her

first day back at school. She imagined sweeping into the pavilion in her new blue dress and dazzling everyone. Being late was not in her plan.

Lindsey looked at the guard's name tag. "Officer Jones, you seem like a nice guy. If I had known there would be a...barrier," Lindsey said, glancing pointedly at the red arm still stretched in front of her bumper, "I would have been early. Couldn't you just accidentally hit the button that raises that thing on your way to the bathroom or something?"

He shook his head.

Lindsey nodded gravely and glanced again at the dashboard clock. She would never make it if she had to go back home, park, and get a cab. "Okay, Jones. What do you like? Chocolate? Booze? I'm not above bribery."

"Clearly," he said, looking at her with amused, but unwavering, eyes.

"I'd even do Sox tickets," she continued, "but please, don't say you like baseball because I really can't afford them."

"Good thing for you and your pocket-book the answer is still no."

Lindsey exhaled. "You're going to make me pull out the big guns now."

"Can't wait."

She looked up at the guard with her doll-like face and smiled. "Okay, here goes: pretty please? Pretty please with sprinkles on top. Sprinkles! Come on, Jones, who can turn down sprinkles?" she said. "I promise I'll move my car as soon as the President's Tea is over."

"I appreciate the effort," he said. "But, no. I'm one year from retirement and a well-earned pension. Can't risk it. It's my ass."

Lindsey felt the air go out of her body. "I understand."

Officer Jones stood back with his hands hitched into his belt, his head tilted to the side. "There is some paid parking on Constitution and Third, it's the closest you'll find, but still a hike," Jones continued. "Not much student parking near here. Most of the kids take public transportation if they don't live on campus."

"You could tell I was a student, huh?"

He smiled. "You might be a bit more put together than some, but the nerves gave you away. I've been here a long time, though, and I'll tell you —not everyone gets invited to that fancy tea. If you're one of them, I don't think you have much to worry about."

"I don't know about that," she said.

"Don't beat yourself up, kid. Tomorrow's another day."

"It's Lindsey," she said, reaching her hand out the window.

He shook her hand, his bulldog eyes crinkling at the corners. "Sorry, Lindsey."

"Don't be sorry, Jones. It's not all bad. At least I

made a new friend, right?"

Jones laughed. "I guess so."

"Alright, Jones. See you around. I'll go find that lot now."

Jones lifted the gate for her to turn around and raised his substantial hand in a cheerful wave. Lindsey hit the gas and pulled forward into the roundabout, then lurched to a sudden stop as a group of students popped up in the crosswalk. The car behind her slammed on its brakes as its horn bellowed. One of the students flipped her off. Lindsey gave Jones an embarrassed shrug, waved to the students in apology and pulled away. Suddenly, she questioned the judgment of the university for offering her an escalated program based on her "experience and potential." If they could see her now, they might change their minds.

She drove as fast as she dared past the cramped historic buildings that lined the nearby streets. Statues and high-rises flew by, all squeezed together through a maze of indecipherable one way streets that changed direction without warning. Boston was a series of contradictions, and Lindsey guessed she was one of them.

Just as she was about to give up and consult a map, the lot appeared at the top of the hill. She took a sharp breath as she pulled in, trying to convince herself it was excitement more than fear she felt as she parked and gathered her things. She thought of her best friend, Kate. Brave Kate who beat the odds and found her American Dream and true love by taking a chance.

Lindsey opened her car door and looked out at the expanse of buildings glowing a fresh sherbet orange in the setting Boston sun. She had waited a decade for this. She ripped the price tag off her dress and threw it in a ball toward her passenger seat. "It's never too late," she whispered to herself as she started walking. "I got this."

Chapter 2: Zach

Zach's gaze drifted across the courtyard to the ripples of light bouncing off the Charles River. A light breeze cut a series of hypnotic wedges into the water, and he could feel the shards of sunlight pulling him away. In the shadows, a lone rower sliced through the water in a single-man skull. Zach felt the muscles in his arms and back tighten as he watched it glide by. His hands gripped an invisible oar at his side.

"Professor Wheeler?"

Zach looked down and felt himself swing back involuntarily. Dean Cruz stood before him, staring intently through overly painted eyes.

"My God," she murmured, "you are easily distracted."

Zach sighed. *How long had she been standing there?* "Just enjoying the day, Dean."

"Yes, I can see that," she clucked, "over here by yourself. Why don't you mingle? Chat up some of our donors?"

"I'll leave that to you. You're the pro."

"Flattery," she said as she moved closer, constricting the air between them. Zach's back arched as he tried to lean even further away. He was close enough now to see the dark red streaks of lipstick that had seeped like oil into the corners of her mouth.

"You are adorable," she said, her fingers reaching up to trace an invisible line down his lapel. "I'll forgive you for standing here by yourself, dazed, but only if you tell me you were creating a workable code in that *big*, big brain of yours."

Zach raised his cocktail and took a sip. "No need for concern," he answered, putting his glass firmly between them, hoping to widen the gap. "We are making progress."

"So you say, Professor. So you always say."

Zach took a deep breath, preparing himself for the same conversation he and the dean had every time she saw him. "Results take time."

The dean tapped the tip of a nail against her wine glass. "Look around," she said. "See all of this?"

Zach scanned the courtyard and nodded. "I do."

"Impressive, isn't it?" she said, looking out at the crowd. "Do you think I get extra time to find funding every year? Including funding for your budget-crippling program?" She did not give him time to respond. "Oh, no," she continued. "I don't get more time. And neither do you."

Zach's eyes widened. "Meaning?"

"Meaning, I've gone out on a limb for you. Four years is a long time."

He scanned her face, hoping to see some hint that she was joking. She looked at him directly, pulling her lips into a tight line. A moment went by as he chose his words. "I'm sure this year we'll have a breakthrough," he said carefully.

"You'd better. There are other demands for the funds I've squandered on you, and you just keep asking for more."

"More? I thought you turned down my request for faster cabling."

"I'm referring to the approval of Ms. Monahan. Where is she, by the way? I was looking forward to seeing this amazing new talent that warranted yet another break in protocol."

Zach cast his eyes to the check-in table. He had put Lindsey's name-tag in the upper right corner so he could keep tabs on when she appeared. It sat alone against the blue tablecloth, untouched. He rubbed his brow. "She'll be here.

"Don't make me regret accepting her."

"She's talented."

"Perhaps, but offering a degree for one year of work is unorthodox. What will I say to your colleagues when they ask for similar...

concessions?"

Zach ground his teeth. "She has the credits. And we need her."

"Alright," she said. "Just please, don't tell me you brought on another weird hacker who can't manage to be in public."

Zach tensed. All he knew were weird hackers who couldn't manage to be in public. If the dean knew what they knew, she would feel the same. "Our work-product will speak for itself."

She smiled, toying with the thick diamond pendant that hung from her neck. "Well, let's hope so, but this better not be some ploy to keep your funding going."

Zach leveled his eyes on hers. "Until today, I didn't know my funding was in danger."

"Of course it is," she said, swirling her drink in her hand. "There is competition in the university for dollars, you know that. I'll do my best to help you — if you deliver results — but I can't make promises."

"You can't make promises?" Zach practically hissed. "I've promised my team that their place is solid for the rest of this year. Are you saying that could change?"

The dean curled her mouth smugly and shrugged. "I need some quid pro quo here, Professor. If I come through for you, will you come through for me?"

Zach met her gaze for a moment, growing increasingly uncomfortable beneath her stare. He looked out beyond her shoulder and saw a diversion. "President Sanders!" Zach called out.

Zach watched as the president of the university turned around in circles, looking left, then right, trying to pinpoint where the voice had come from. When he saw Zach waving at him, a wide grin spread beneath his whiskers. He waddled over on his wooden cane and turned directly to Zach.

"Professor Wheeler! Good to see you, sir," he said, patting Zach on the shoulder. "And you, Dean," he said with a sideways glance.

"I assume you've seen the fund-raising roster?" Dean Cruz asked the president. "Fifteen percent higher than last fall already."

"Yes, yes," the president mumbled. "Very impressive." He coughed. "I noticed," he said, looking around, "that you took the liberty of inviting some of your donors to my tea. I must say, that is...bold, Dean Cruz."

"Our contributors are business people," she answered blithely. "They want to see a return on their investment. Introducing them to our young talent is just the type of exposure that will increase their contributions."

"We've already hit our goals this year," the president said, "why not leave the students this one space to thrive without scrutiny, hmm?"

The dean let out a clipped laugh, as if a tiny bird was trying to escape from her throat. "I know the education of our bright young minds is paramount to you, President Sanders, but fund raising is my domain. We have a valuable commodity to offer our contributors, whether that be taking credit for new innovation or putting their name on a building."

"Maybe they just want to support good work," Zach blurted, his blood pressure rising. "Maybe people just want to —"

"That is a nice idea," interrupted the dean. "If only the world worked that way. Lucky for the university, I do the fund raising. You stick to the research."

Zach felt the muscles in his neck tense as the dean raised an eyebrow and glared at him. Zach turned back toward President Sanders, hoping for a reprieve, but he had already lost interest in the conversation, his eyes wandering to the far corners of the room. Zach took his phone out of his pocket. "I have to take this," he said, pretending it had been buzzing. "If you'll excuse me."

Zach made his way up to a stone patio. The farther he got from the dean, the better he felt. He took a look down at the courtyard and the many faces meandering by with drinks in their hands. To Zach's dismay, it was only about half students. He watched as groups of business people gathered in small circles, shaking hands and gossiping over their free cheese and cocktails. Zach squeezed his eyes together and took a breath. Twenty years in academia and he still hated these functions. He reminded himself it was the nature of the beast. His research didn't pay for itself, after all.

As he opened his eyes again, he saw three familiar students wave in his direction. They were each blond, with a penchant for staring and twirling their hair. He wondered if they had actually gotten an invitation to the President's Tea…or if they were crashing, as usual. Fashion students didn't usually attend science events. At least this time they hadn't cornered him. He put his phone to his ear and turned away as he dialed.

"Hey, bro," his brother, Sam, answered on the third ring.

"Save me."

"Oh, no. Not another campus event you need to sneak away from?"

Zach groaned. "You nailed it. These people make my skin crawl. If I could just stay in the lab and never have to deal with people, I'd be happy."

"Why don't you?"

"Politics. Plus, I had a new student that was supposed to be here. She was a no-show."

"Wow. You can pick 'em. Sounds like your love life."

"Very funny. Not all of us want to be a lothario, Samuel."

"Don't knock it till you try it." He laughed. "Besides, aren't you surrounded by twenty-year old hotties? You could use the old professor-student logic. Teach them something valuable they can take out into the world. You'd like that."

Zach looked back at the three fashion students, their eyes still cutting his way. One was actually pulling her cocktail straw in and out of her mouth as she smiled. "Not my style," he said. "I don't have time for that anyway."

"I know, I know, all you care about is saving the world in your own geeky way. But seriously, even you have to blow off some steam now and then."

"If I hurry, I can still make it out to row tonight before it's totally dark."

"Rowing? Seriously?" He heard his brother exhale. "Zachary, listen to me, life goes by in a snap. You are going to miss it. You row every morning on that stupid river. Tonight, go out and get laid."

Zach smiled. That was his brother's solution to everything. Sometimes he wished things could be that simple. "Nah, I appreciate the advice though."

"Okay, Zach. Do your thing. By the way, I'll be out on a case for a few weeks. Don't be worried if I don't answer your calls for a while."

"Top secret, again?"

"Like always."

"Okay, Sam. Be safe."

They hung up and Zach looked over the courtyard and the shadows that began to stretch across the patio in the dimming light. He ditched his cocktail and darted toward the entrance. Lindsey's name-tag still sat unmoved on the table. He turned and scanned the room; almost everyone was gone. He felt a sudden surge of panic. What if she had changed her mind? He was close to creating a code that would change the world and Lindsey Monahan might be the missing piece that could make his dream a reality...before the dean pulled his funding for good. He had to find her.

If it wasn't too late, he might be able to catch someone at Campus Housing that could tell him which dorm they had put her in. He lurched forward and began to sprint out of the Tea and across the quad.

Chapter 3: Lindsey

Lindsey tucked her short hair behind her ears and leaned against a warm stone wall outside the pavilion to catch her breath. Bending to the side, she tried in vain to dust some of the dirt from her bare feet before forcing her high heels back on. *Hobble in and smile*, she told herself. "Hello, I'm Lindsey Monahan," she murmured, practicing for the hundredth time as she rounded the side of the building to enter the pavilion. It took her eyes a moment to adjust to the warm, afternoon glow that bounced off the water, bathing the courtyard in a soft, pink haze. Her eyes darted back and forth; everyone was gone.

"Dammit, Lindsey," she cursed, wincing as she made her way to a nearby chair. She pried off the two torture devices stuck to her feet and felt the skin on her heels swell as they hit the open air.

She tried to let the warmth of the setting sun dry the tears welling behind her eyes. Clearly, she sucked at first impressions. If only the world was like code, she thought, then she could go back and rewrite this whole day. She would be confident, beautiful, brilliant...and on time. Her breath caught in her throat as she warmed to the fantasy, and again, she rewound to the beginning and practiced uselessly what she would have said, and who she would have met, when she suddenly heard giggling to her right. She opened one eye and peeked sideways toward the sound.

Three college aged girls were gathered around a side table, all dropping their weight onto one hip in a perfect expression of boredom. Their blond hair and outfits were impeccable and effortless, as if they were in competition for who could be the most girly-girl ever.

One held a giant silver flask with both tiny hands as another deftly poured the half empty wine bottles from the catering table into it. The third was wrapping bits of cheese in a napkin and shoving it in her purse. "Hurry up, you guys," shrieked the third. "The cleaning crew is coming!"

"Calm down, Heather," said the first, looking over to a group of workers in coveralls walking across the quad. "Like these people care if we swipe university leftovers."

"Oh," said the second, also looking at the crew. "Leave some for them. I bet they make shit money."

As the third girl scanned the room, she caught Lindsey's eye and stopped. "Hold up. We may have a problem."

All three turn toward Lindsey and stared at her with their over-sized eyes. Lindsey sat up and tucked in her feet. She must look a mess.

One of the three raised her head in a nod. "Hi there," she offered, "you here for the Tea?"

"Yes," Lindsey called back, curling her bare toes further beneath her chair. "But I guess I missed it."

"You just got here?" asked girl number two. "Then, yeah. You totally missed it."

"Yeah," agreed girl number three.

"Stop," said Heather, raising her hand. "You didn't miss anything. It was heinous." She hesitated. "You a student...or a teacher?"

"Who, me?" asked Lindsey. "I'm a student. Kind of."

Heather looked her over then shrugged as if the whole conversation was becoming too boring. "Well, the only good thing about these stupid teas is that there's free wine and cheese to help us kick off our Friday night party."

"Pre-party, bitches!" called out girl number two, holding up her fist for a bump that never came.

"What are you studying?" Girl number three asked Lindsey.

"Um, I'm working on a special project...at the computer lab."

"Ooh!" cried out girl number two, "do you have Professor Wheeler?" The other two girls snapped their necks back toward the conversation.

"Yeah. Guess I missed him." Lindsey shrugged. "Bonehead move."

The three gathered up the rest of their haul and made their way over to Lindsey, ready to talk. Each had her own perfectly styled hair and makeup, looking more like they were on a trip to Vegas than a campus Tea. They were each adorable in a sexy kind of way that left Lindsey both impressed and perplexed. She vaguely thought she would need a scuba tank to breath in any one of their outfits.

Heather stepped toward Lindsey and leveled a look at her as if she was going to say something epically important. "I'm Heather," she said. "This is Brie, and that's Taylor." The other girls nodded at Lindsey, then looked back at Heather, who shot her hand in the air like she was about to yell *hallelujah!* "Wheeler," she said, "is hot."

"Hot!" agreed Brie.

"Smoking," added Taylor.

"He's the only thing pretty enough to look at on the faculty," Heather continued. "But don't even bother. All the girls have tried."

"I more than tried," added Brie. "I brought my A-game, but he still shot me down. Me!" she added, shaking her head.

"Yeah," chimed Taylor. "Hot, but shoots all the girls down." She raised her hand up like a gun.

"Ping! Ping! Toast. No chance."

"Whatevs," said Heather. "He has a computer chip stuck up his ass. Like," she moved her arms up and down like a robot, "no girls, no fun, does not compute."

The other girls laughed, then tossed their hair to signal this part of the conversation was over.

"Anyway," Heather turned to Lindsey, "what's your name?"

"Lindsey."

"Uh-huh," said Heather, scanning Lindsey up and down. "You're cute. Want to come to a frat party with us?"

Lindsey looked back at their bored, pretty faces and felt suddenly and totally out of place. "Thanks, but I have plans." *Plans unpacking and burying my sorrows in a bag of chips*, she thought to herself.

"Okay, Lindsey," Heather said, and all three shrugged. "Enjoy the computer lab, then."

Lindsey's stomach felt suddenly hollow as she watched the three girls sway effortlessly out of the pavilion. She imagined their college days were full of fun, parties, friends, and sex. All of the things she had missed. Lindsey grabbed her shoes by the heel and made her way out into the quad.

It was Friday night, and she could hear laughter and music playing in the distance; not so far away, she saw smiling people slicing through the crowds on bicycles, anxious to get wherever they were going. Lindsey sighed. As usual, she didn't fit in. Maybe this was all a terrible idea.

Lindsey pulled out her phone and called her mom. Usually, on a Friday night, the two of them would be curled up under Afghans just starting a movie. If they were really in a crazy mood, they would share a frozen cherry cheesecake eaten straight out of the box. Her call went to voice mail. What could her mom possibly be doing? She had put on a brave face this morning as Lindsey pulled away, but Lindsey knew her mom would miss her. She was probably doing laundry and couldn't hear the phone ring.

Lindsey hesitated, then scrolled down to Kate. It was only day one and she already needed Kate to hold her hand. Oh well, what were best friends for?

"Hey, Kate. You around?" Lindsey texted.

Immediately her phone lit up. "Lindz! How's the big city? How's your first day?"

"Awful," Lindsey replied. "I screwed up already. Maybe this college thing really isn't for me."

There was a moment before a response popped up. "What are you talking about? Of course this is for you! You are Lindsey freaking Monahan. That university doesn't know who it's messing with, right?"

Lindsey didn't respond, and a moment later her phone lit up again. "Right? Right, Lindz?"

"Sure," Lindsey wrote back.

"I know this is all new," Kate texted, "but

that's the best part! Remember, nobody there knows you! You can totally reinvent yourself. You can decide who you want to be!"

Lindsey smiled at the screen and began to text back. "Secret agent? Famous magician?"

"All that and more."

Lindsey held tightly to her phone and looked out over the flowing water of the Charles River and the newly glistening lights of the Boston skyline. Kate was right. Monday, she would be in the lab—that's when her new life would really start. She wasn't going to give up this easily. Tonight was her first night on her own, and she was going to enjoy herself.

Chapter 4: Zach

Zach stood in the doorway a moment to test the motion sensor. A red light blinked from the camera to his right as a crackling sound bit through the silence of the lab. Soft blue lights soaked the lab in a cool haze, interrupted only by the occasional click of a router or screen saver that bounced light across the floor. His eyes adjusted quickly, used to the comforting dim light of the lab more than the incandescent light that flooded the hallway outside.

He let the door shut quietly behind him, scanning how each chair was positioned, each mouse. Nothing seemed to be out of place—at least, not tonight. Satisfied, he locked the heavy steel door behind him and hit the master switch on the control panel to his left.

A pale yellow light fixture crackled to life, bathing the far corners of the room in an antiseptic, industrial light more accustomed to an aging hospital than the national epi-center of data science in the country—just the way Zach liked it.

He took ten steps directly to the corner and placed his palm flat against a giant locked door. He could feel the vibration of the monster-sized servers crammed into the room within. He gazed down at the lock; he could see no tampering.

Satisfied, he pulled off his jacket and made his way across the square linoleum tiles of the floor toward the door of his adjacent office. He flipped through a second set of keys, each unlocking another section of the door before it swung open to reveal the cramped, dark room within. Five blinking screens were stacked expertly atop the desk, a sliver of light bouncing through one screen then up into another.

He threw his jacket across the back of his desk chair before plopping down into the seat and leaning back. His long legs stretched out below the desk as he raised his arms above his head. He took a deep breath and listened to the click and whir of the systems around him. Again, he inhaled, hoping he could unclench his hands and stop temptation from washing over him.

He exhaled, and took another breath before opening his eyes and glancing at his keyboard. It would be easy to break into the campus housing server and get the information he needed on Lindsey Monahan. Then, at least, he could get her cell and make sure she was coming to the lab Monday morning. After all, he ran all the way to their office in the stifling Boston heat, only to find they had shut the doors seven minutes early. Some people lived nine-to-five lives. Well, in this case, nine-to-4:53, apparently. He couldn't blame them, really. It was Friday afternoon and they probably wanted to get home.

He put the toe of his shoe decisively against the desk and pushed his chair back across the linoleum. *You made the rules,* he told himself, *you can't break them. No hacking.*

He twirled around in his chair and tried to relax before giving up and trudging the few steps toward his coffee maker. It sat above a mini-fridge tucked in next to a single bed, still half full with the remainder of this morning's brew. He pulled it out and swished the waxy black liquid around in the pot, bringing it up to his nose. It smelled bitter, but like it still might get the job done. He turned the power on to warm up the remnants, then fell onto the bed and rested his feet against the wall.

His Delta Project had made huge strides in Big Data Coding in its young four years. Just getting the project started, explaining it so other people understood it and supported it, was a miraculous endeavor. But explaining it wasn't enough. There was a wave coming, and Zach had to get ahead of it. Information traveled through wires and satellites in a flash, and soon, the crackling terminals in his lab would be relics. Technology was charging forward. Disparate information flew through the ether, and whoever could harness those separate pieces of data, and read it in one language, would change the world forever — for better, or worse.

As he stared at the ceiling, he noticed a water stain that had crept across the graying tile above his bed. He would get a ladder and check out the source tomorrow. He didn't want campus engineers poking around in here.

He sat up and looked out at the lab where an empty work station had been built just outside his door, ready for his new coder. Well, hacker was more accurate, but Lindsey Monahan was clearly an expert coder, or she never could have gotten through his game. He felt anticipation bubble in his chest as he thought about Monday morning. He murmured a silent wish that she was, in fact, the missing piece that would bring everything together.

It was clear last month that the project had stalled. The team had created roads of code, each wandering toward a single destination, only to dead-end before connecting. None of them could configure a path forward. He needed a fresh set of eyes. So, last month he put an invitation in the back pages of a computer magazine, inviting coders to play a series of games, each designed to discover competitors with a particular skill-set. Scores took up the challenge, and a couple even reached the end, but Lindsey Monahan was totally different.

She poked around in the first two games, clearly testing his code, then built a tunnel under the program and hopped directly to the end. She won — not by playing, but by rebuilding the game from the inside out. None of the other players even thought of doing that. He hadn't even thought of doing that. He didn't even realize she had done it until he received a note inside the game that read, *"What else?"*

Zach flushed with adrenaline as he deconstructed what she had done. She could be the answer he was searching for, but someone this talented could also be dangerous. He jumped online and tried to find her trail, some bread-crumbs he could follow to find out who she was and what she was after. She went by the moniker Viper; beyond that, he found nothing. He brought in his team, they also found nothing.

Then, one night, as he was playing on his PS4, a Viper popped up on the screen. "I'm bored," she said. "Can I play?"

Blood drained from his face as he stared at her words. Hacking into a multi-player system was supposed to be impossible. Anyone who could do that was a genius. He needed a genius. His fingers flew to the keyboard. "Want to play?" he responded. "Be on my team."

Admission to the Delta Project meant he would find out who she was. When he got a pop-up that her transcripts had arrived, he ran to his desk and couldn't get the file to open fast enough. Viper was Lindsey Monahan. Clearly a prodigy who skipped the second and third grades, got a perfect SAT score in math and started at a prominent university at sixteen. Then, six months later, she dropped out and disappeared into the dark, anonymous coils of the virtual world. She left no trace after that, no social media presence, no work history, not a bread crumb to follow. She had, however, taken enough on-line courses all over the world that she could have gotten three advanced degrees by now. That was the one thing that helped him understand this virtual ghost. She wanted an education; she wanted a degree. With that, he convinced the dean to give her a full ride and a degree for joining his team full-time for a year. He had something she wanted, and she had something he needed. A dangerous, but necessary proposition.

His phone buzzed in his pocket. His face fell in the dim light of the screen as he read a text from Dean Cruz.

"We need to continue our conversation. Be at my office at 2pm tomorrow. We must discuss expectations for the remainder of the year."

Zach tossed his phone into the pile of sheets wadded up in the corner of bed. The dean was never satisfied with the bits of data he had been giving her to keep the dollars flowing into the lab. He needed to give her something tangible — and fast. Zach stared again at Lindsey's digital file.

Could she be the key? He wished he could reach into the screen and shake it like a real folder, hoping a new piece of paper would fly out, revealing the answer.

He took a deep breath and closed his eyes. Maybe his brother was right. It was Friday night and he could sit in the lab driving himself crazy, or go have a drink. After all, he would meet his new student Monday and that's when the real work would begin.

Chapter 5: Lindsey

The tips of a buzzing neon light glowed from a sunken stairwell across from Lindsey's apartment. She stood on her tippy-toes and peered into the darkness, where she could just make out the top of a sign that read 'cold beer.' She dropped back to the concrete and stood for a moment before turning around. She craned her neck and looked up to the third floor of her new building where her living room window remained dark and silent. *Quiet up there*, she thought. She bit her lip and swung the high-heels that dangled from her fingertips as she considered her options. *New life*, she reminded herself, and walked toward the sign.

She clutched an iron rail as she made her way down a crumbling concrete staircase into the sunken entrance to the bar. As she opened the door, the smell of rotted wood and years of stale cigarette smoke engulfed her. The light from the street cast her shadow far across the boards that lined the floor.

A bartender looked her way. "Coming or going?" he asked.

Lindsey took a step in and let the old door swing shut behind her, cutting off the last of the outside air.

"Coming, I guess."

Lindsey's eyes adjusted and swept the room. A puffy, older lady sat in the corner, stirring an empty glass with a single, plastic straw. Across from her, a man slept, his head buried in his arms. The bartender slid slowly off his chair and limped over to the bar-top, rag in hand. This is not what Lindsey imagined when she mustered the courage to come inside.

"What are you having?" asked the bartender, his crooked nose hanging loosely above an equally crooked smirk.

Lindsey looked at the rows of bottles stacked on the wall behind him. Her eyes landed on a warped 1970's poster for Tequila Sunrise. An amber, ice-filled glass was nestled against silky, golden grains of sand. Suddenly, she felt a million miles from her childhood home in Worcester and the hideous President's Tea. "Tequila," she said. "Sunrise."

The bartender shrugged as if he didn't approve, but turned away and filled a glass with ice. As he did, Lindsey placed her heels on the floor beneath a bar stool and hopped up onto its flattened, peeling leather. *At least I don't have to go home and look at all of those boxes*, she thought.

The bartender frisbeed a twisted cardboard coaster onto the bar and placed her drink on top of it, which stopped it from spinning. She pulled the drink toward her. Nestled in the shards of ice floated one booze soaked cherry. She picked it up by the stem and placed it on the bar. It rolled drunkenly to its side and stopped there. *That sounds good*, she thought. *Join You? Don't mind if I do.* She downed the drink and signaled to the bartender for another. As the next drink came, she settled back into her chair. *This was her life*, she thought. *Not young enough for College, not old enough to make friends with the drunk in the corner.*

Lindsey thought about tomorrow and the task of unloading all of her boxes. The only thing she had managed to unpack was her computer equipment; she couldn't keep her babies stifled inside a stuffy cardboard box. As for the rest, she didn't know where to begin. She had lived in her mom's basement for so long she had never thought about how to organize a new place. *I'll think about that tomorrow*, she thought as the drinks and cherries piled up. *Tonight, I'm in a new place, and I'm going to celebrate,* she told herself as she arranged her new collection of cherries into a smiley face, the mouth stuck together with toothpicks. The face smiled back at her awkwardly, its crooked mouth mocking her.

Party of one! She smiled to herself. *Will nothing ever change?*

A rush of air sucked out of the room as the door opened behind her. The bartender slid off his chair and began to pour Jameson into a glass with two cubes of ice. He nodded at the newcomer. "Long time," he said as he placed the glass two seats down from Lindsey.

In the reflection of the bar mirrors, she glimpsed the tall silhouette of the man. As he strode forward, she could make out a stoic expression and broad shoulders highlighted by the tailoring of a dark jacket. Lindsey shifted and heard the leather beneath her crackle. Her eyes stayed fixed on the bar as the man removed his jacket and slid onto his chair. Lindsey sipped the last, watery liquid from her glass and set it back on the bar, the melting ice cubes falling into the bottom with a clink. A moment passed, then, without turning toward her, the man spoke.

"Bad shoes?" he asked.

Lindsey looked down at her dangling, bare feet. "Nah," she answered, laughing. "The shoes are fine. It's my feet. They just don't fit right."

She watched as a smile spread across his face in the distorted reflection of the bar mirror. He didn't respond, so she kept talking.

"I walked a long way today," she continued, "just to get nowhere."

"I can relate," he said, his eyes raising slowly to

meet hers over the bottles of booze.

Even through the faded, milky glass, she felt a tremor run through her. She forced herself to swallow. "You can?" she asked. "Well that makes us friends then!"

"I guess it does," he replied, turning his chair toward her.

Lindsey swiveled and met his gaze across an empty bar stool. She was startled by the intensity of his eyes, incongruous with the sun-kissed skin and hair that surrounded them, but deep within the blue, she saw a kindness she hadn't expected. His lips parted as if he wanted to say something impulsive, something intimate. He gripped the side of the bar with a large, tanned hand and spoke without his eyes leaving hers. She felt her mouth water, but willed her face to remain still.

"What's she drinking?" he asked the bartender.

"Tequila," the bartender said.

"That sounds about right," the man said. "Two, Rick."

The bartender lumbered over and tossed a soiled bar towel across his shoulder. "Straight, or with wheels?"

Lindsey felt her brow tighten in confusion.

"Wheels," answered the man. "Thanks."

The bartender slapped two shot glasses on the bar and filled them with a dark, amber liquid. Beside the glasses, he placed a cocktail napkin with two limes.

Lindsey watched the man as he reached for his tequila, his arms straining the fabric of his button-down shirt. She picked up her own shot in one hand and the lime in the other, then tipped the glass to her lips in an effort not to stare. She was just about to lick the salt from the rim of her glass when the man spoke again.

"We're doing it wrong," he whispered.

"What's that?" She turned her face back toward his.

Two perfect dimples formed on either side of his lips as he spoke. "Aren't friends supposed to sit together?"

Lindsey swallowed. *Holy hottness.* She remembered Kate's advice, and of all the things she'd never done, like have shots with a handsome stranger. Her hand landed with a slap on the bar stool to her right. She rubbed the leather in a slow circle. "It's all yours, friend."

The man slid his shot down the bar and moved closer. As he sat, Lindsey felt the air surrounding her ignite. She felt the need to fan herself, but raised the shot to her lips instead, hoping the warm brown liquid would soothe her. She downed the tequila and cooled her lips with a bite of lime.

"No lime and salt for you?" muttered Lindsey, turning her eyes up toward the smooth skin of his face.

"I'm not a training wheels kind of a guy," he answered, his eyes dropping to hers.

"And I am? What gave me away?"

"Your other friend," he answered, pointing down at her cherry smiley-face. "You'd better hide the evidence, though, or Rick will stop serving you."

"Oops," Lindsey answered, looking down. "Good point." She began to disassemble the cherries, then stopped. "But how can I get rid of this guy?" she asked. "We've been through so much together…"

"I'll keep you company," said Zach, "if you want…"

Lindsey felt her pulse quicken. "Oh," she gulped, "I do."

"What's your name?" he asked, looking intently into her eyes.

Lindsey uncrossed then re-crossed her legs, remembering what Kate said about reinventing herself. Now was as good a time as any. "My name?" Lindsey responded. "That's boring."

"Your name is boring?"

"No, silly, the question is." She swirled her fingertip across the patterns in the bar. "Besides, I'm a secret agent, don't tell anyone."

"I see. Well then, don't hurt me, Agent."

Lindsey took a breath of the warm air surrounding them. "There are several things I can think of doing to you, friend," she said, trailing her finger up along his hand to his forearm. "Hurting you isn't one of them." Her mouth ran dry, stunned at herself. She tried to swallow and groped for what remained of her shot.

The man leaned closer, his hand now grazing the silky material covering her thigh. "Are you trying to seduce me?" he asked.

Lindsey felt her skin catch fire beneath his. "Maybe," she whispered.

"Because if you are, keep doing it," he said, leaning in. "I've been watching your mouth since we've been sitting here, and, well—it's pretty fucking amazing."

Lindsey felt herself drift suddenly into the woody, sweet smell of his neck. *Maybe this day isn't a total disaster after all,* she told herself as she watched the man throw several bills on the bar and turn toward her. He bent forward, the muscles in his chest and pants straining as he stared unabashed at the pucker of her bottom lip.

Between the rapid beats of her heart she managed to speak. "Let's get out of here," she said.

Chapter 6: Zach

The moment Zach opened the door to the bar, he saw the back of her neck, long and pale, and framed perfectly by tiny, brown curls of hair. He stopped mid-step—same door, same bartender, same bar. He wasn't in the wrong place, he had just never seen a woman like this here before.

As the door shut behind him, the room sank farther into darkness, but her skin still radiated through the chalky neon light. He stared at the alabaster, shining quality of it as he moved past her. The soft cream of her shoulders begged to be removed from the folds of dark blue fabric that draped over them. He clenched his house keys in his fist as he walked past in an effort not to reach out and glide his finger across her.

Maybe his brother was right—he did need to get laid. He had not reacted to the presence of a woman like this in a long, long time.

There was an empty chair just beside her, but he decided not to take it. That would be too obvious. Instead, he slid onto a stool two seats down. He waited for his drink before venturing a sideways glance. She sat alone, her back straight, her two perfect feet curled naked beneath her bar stool. Even her ankles glowed pale and white as if they had been carved out of snowflakes, and as he glanced at her in the reflection of the bar mirror, he saw two huge doll-like eyes staring back at him between the dusty bottles of booze that lined the wall. He looked away and downed his Jameson to steady himself.

What she was doing in his bar, he did not know, but Zach didn't believe in coincidence. He felt there must be some synchronicity at work, a reason that she landed here on the one night he came in and sat beside her—like some mathematical equation lying just below the surface that made everything feel perfectly right. Or, maybe it was lust. He couldn't tell. As his mind toppled with possibilities, he ordered another drink.

He glanced again to his left. She looked like a ballerina, her arms and fingers stretched delicately against the aging wood of the bar, her head angled to reveal a perfect soft line of flesh that ran across her clavicle. Her lips were a delicate pink, and he wondered if that was a natural flush or lipstick. He wanted to kiss her and find out. She was a woman, and her presence reminded him there were people out in the world, people he could reach out and touch—if he was lucky.

Then his eyes slid to the bar where she had arranged a row of cocktail cherries into a lopsided face. He let out a small gasp of surprise. She had positioned the shiny red balls so the stems created eyebrows and the mouth curved in a cartoonish, toothy grin. She just wanted a drink and a smile. Well, several drinks and a smile from the looks of it. He found the delight of it more intoxicating than his drink. Then, when she smiled and asked him to sit beside her, he felt his shoulders sink down and long pent up tension slide completely away.

Now, he had her by the hand, pulling her through the warm Boston air and across the street to his building. They darted past an old street lamp to the dark, cool recesses of the historic stone facade just below his stoop. There, he stopped and laced his fingers through hers and took a breath. She was looking up at him with her big, expectant brown eyes, her lips slightly parted, waiting for what would come next. He steadied himself through the increasingly rapid beats of his heart, wanting to savor every moment he had with this unexpected woman.

He looked at her for a long, delicious moment before slowly pulling her arms up around his neck. He bent his head toward hers and leaned her gently against the wall, touching just the edge of his lips to hers. As he did, he felt her mouth open and her tongue brush against his. Such a shock of pleasure went through him that he felt himself sway slightly. Blood rushed through his limbs and groin and he steadied himself by pressing against her. He lowered his lips and layered soft kisses from just below her ear down toward her breast, feeling her pulse quicken beneath the surface of her skin.

The fine bones of her hands moved against the muscles of his lower back, urging him even closer. The small mounds of her breasts pushed up against him, his groin swelling thick and hard against her belly. He felt her writhe, heat and moisture pressing into his leg.

Zach took a breath and squeezed her hand. "Let's go upstairs," he said in her ear. She leaned back and nodded quickly, the flush of her skin evident in the light of the full, summer moon.

He took her by the hand and made his way up the front stoop of his building, fumbling with his keys. Beside him, he heard her release a soft giggle.

"What?" he turned and asked.

"Nothing," she answered, her eyes wide.

The door swung open, and as it did, Zach grabbed her by the hand and pulled her up the stairs. When they reached the second floor, she pulled him by the hand toward the staircase.

"What?" he asked again.

"Come on," she said, and pulled him up another flight. As they reached the landing of the third floor, she fell back against a door and coyly dangled a set of keys in her hand.

He blinked as the surprise set in. "No…" he said.

"Uh huh," she said with a tentative smile.

"You live here?"

"Uh huh."

"What? When — ?" he began, but she turned and pushed him gently against the door, then curled her hand around the back of his neck, kissing him again.

He felt his body flush in response, even as he let out a small laugh. Of course she lived here. Who else would go to Rick's? She pressed her hands flat against his chest, pushing him against the door of her apartment. While she kissed him, she worked her small hand behind his back. As he heard her key turn in the lock, his body ignited.

The two tumbled through the open door, and Zach barely caught them both before they landed in a mass on the floor. They took only a beat to steady themselves before pulling at each other's clothes. Her hands undid the buttons of his shirt, then slid across his chest, her fingers sliding softly against his nipples. He grasped at the shoulders of her dress and slowly pulled it down her arms and torso until it fell in a pile at her feet. His hands slid across the lace of her bra as he looked at her, then he curled his thumbs through the straps and pulled the bra away from her skin, revealing her perfect breasts and nipples. Breath escaped him as he stroked one nipple with the pad of his thumb. "My God, you *are* soft," he murmured as he took her breast in his mouth.

The scent of her skin was so clean and velvety he wanted to melt right into her. He bent down and curled his hand around the back of her thighs, then lifted her up in one smooth motion so she straddled his waist. Her tiny torso perched there, her taut, glistening nipples shining in the dark just in front of his lips. As he licked her, she curled her long legs around him and arched her back, making their bodies meet as a slow rhythm built between them.

She threw her arms tightly around his neck as the tempo of their movements grew, and she whispered something so quietly into his ear he could barely make it out. It sounded like, 'Oh my God, I can't believe this is happening'. His hands gripped her hungrily as her words sank in. He felt the same, and he pushed himself as close to her as he could with his pants still on. He needed this. He wanted this.

As if she could sense what he was thinking, she pulled back. "Take those off," she said, tugging at his waist.

He picked her up gently and placed her beside him, then stood, pulling at his belt. He grinned. "I'm so glad I met you."

"Me too," she breathed, her eyes gliding down over his body.

"I'm going to do wonderful things to you," he said as his pants dropped to the ground, exposing the long, strong muscles of his legs and a towering erection.

He watched as her eyes took him in. "Me first," she said, dropping to her knees.

She looked up at the glistening, solid length of him before glancing up and meeting his eyes. His breath caught in his throat as she held him by the back of his thighs, then began to caress him gently with her lips and tongue. Her mouth was wet and warm, and each stroke sent a current through his chest, cleansing his mind until it felt blissfully empty. He forgot the lab, and the Charles, Dean Cruz, and the Delta Project. All he thought about was this amazing woman and her tongue, her beautiful skin, and her smile.

He felt his heart swell as his head fell forward and he saw her before him. He reached down to pull her up to take her to the bed when his eyes adjusted slowly to the room. Along each wall and corner were rows of stacked, beige moving boxes. He raised his head and blinked, pulling away from her.

She looked up at him. "What is it?"

He frowned. "You're not leaving, are you?"

Chapter 7: Lindsey

Lindsey trailed soft, light kisses up his torso and onto his open mouth. "What?" she teased as she stood on her toes, wrapping her arms around his neck. "You don't want me to leave?"

Before he could answer, she slid her tongue just inside his lips. His arms tensed, and with two giant hands, he swung her around so he pressed against her from behind, the soft palm of his right hand pulling her back against him. She felt a spark flare within her as his lips began to caress the back of her neck.

"You can't leave," he murmured against the back of her ear. "Not when things are just getting interesting."

Lindsey felt herself fill with a pleasant, wanting liquid. "I'm not," she sputtered, warmth filling her spine. "I'm not moving out. I'm just moving in."

He spun her back around, his beautiful face

glowing at her words. He lifted her like she was nothing and carried her to the sofa. He laid her down and looked at her, his eyes trailing from her mouth to her breasts, then to her delicate lace panties. She wondered if he could sense how wet she was. She hoped that he could.

He lunged forward, laying the length of his body against hers, his skin so warm and solid that her legs spread instinctively beneath him, allowing him to sink even closer.

Her muscles tensed and swelled in anticipation. *Maybe this day wasn't a total bust after all,* she thought absently. Of all the things she had longed to experience in her life, a hook-up with a beautiful stranger wasn't on the list. But now, cradled in this man's arms, his lips and groin pressing against her, she decided this was one new thing she was happy to experience. She heard these one night stands could go from hot to awkward fast, but the way he touched her felt like...well, like love. Maybe she was crazy, but she allowed herself to sink into the moment, the dream of her new life expanding.

She took his handsome face in both of her hands and pulled away to look into his eyes. They were filled with anticipation and longing, but with none of the doubt she would have expected from a man she'd just met. She caressed the strong, golden line of his jaw and smiled. He smiled back and took her hand, kissing the palm as he stared into her eyes. He massaged her breast lightly, then trailed his fingertips down the curve of her belly and beneath her panties, stroking the moist hair between her legs until her thighs began to tremble.

"I could do this all day," he said.

"Okay," Lindsey whispered, her voice begging. In response, his hand slid across her in a slick, rapid motion. She felt herself swell at the thought that he would soon be inside of her. She felt his body tense too, and thought he must be thinking the same thing, until his hand slowed to a stop. He went suddenly still and she realized his eyes were fixed on something across the room. She craned her head to see what he was looking at. She looked across the boxes to the bank of monitors and CPUs she had arranged on the kitchen counter. His body went stiff.

"What?" she asked. "What is it?"

He jumped up from the couch in a shot and began to look around. He turned in circles, his eyes wide.

Lindsey got up onto her knees, pulling a pillow across her naked chest. "You're freaking me out," she whispered.

She watched as he charged across the room to the kitchen where her moving receipt was still laying on the counter, every muscle tightening in his beautiful body as he read it.

He turned toward her, the paper crumpled into his fist. "What the hell is this?"

"Um, my moving receipt. Why?"

He took several long breaths then glared at her, a question in his eyes. His muscles tensed before speaking. "You're good," he said, shaking his head and reaching across the floor to pick up his scattered clothes. "You almost had me."

Lindsey's mouth went slack. "What?"

He turned toward her, his eyes flashing. "You hacked me," he said. "And I actually thought that... that—never mind," he said, shoving his legs into his pants.

Lindsey felt her mouth go dry. "What?" she asked. "I—"

"I'm so stupid," he spat, shaking his head. "Of course, you did." He grabbed his shirt and shoes, his face growing red. "You found out where I lived, moved in, then," his palm slid over his face in one slow, regretful motion, "seduced me." He swung toward her. "Right? Right! Admit it."

"I—"

"Don't deny it," he said. "You hackers and your stupid games. But you," he continued, now pointing at her, "you, Viper, you take things to a whole new level, right? It's not enough to hack me. You had to screw with my head, too."

Lindsey felt a trickle of light begin to seep into her brain. How could he know her moniker was Viper? *Only*—oh no. "Wait," she began, her voice trembling. "You can't be..." She could barely get the words out. "You're Professor Wheeler?"

He stood and looked at her flatly, the veins in

his arms and neck bulging.

"Hah!" he spat. "Like you didn't know that. You waited at that bar. You brought me here!"

"Hold on a minute," Lindsey said, standing with the pillow clutched to her body. "You brought me here, not the other way around."

"Nice try," he said. "Like we just happened to live in the same building."

Lindsey tried to calm her heart rate. She felt her whole life begin to swirl down a dark and irreversible drain as she spoke. "Campus housing put me here," she said slowly. "They said the dorms were full, they —"

"Save it." Zach said as he jerked her front door open. "You're out. Don't you step a foot near my lab."

The door slammed with a bang and Lindsey fell back onto the sofa, listening to Zach's heavy footsteps storm down the stairwell. A moment later, she heard the door to the unit just below hers open and slam fatally shut.

Tears sprung to her eyes. How had this happened? She hadn't even started the program and it was over? Her mind spun through his words, over and over until the doom sunk in. Her dream was over. She curled up around her pillow and sobbed.

She should have just stayed in her mom's basement, safe in a virtual word. That's where she always belonged anyway.

Chapter 8: Zach

Zach felt the back of his hair dry quickly in the summer sun as he stomped across campus. He had paced most of the night before hitting the Charles at dawn. Three lengths of the river up and back tore at the muscles in his arms and back, but did nothing to calm his mind. A permanent groove had dug itself between his clenched eyebrows. He ran his hand through the last damp pieces of his hair and then trailed his palm down roughly over his face before hobbling up the lobby stairs of the dean's office.

This job is aging me, he thought. *But who cares? I should retire anyway. Go into the private sector. Drink myself silly on a beach.* Anything but enduring the constant failure of his project and now his fresh, aching personal failure. He didn't know how he could have been more careful. He was on the verge of paranoia already, but for one night, he let himself go to meet a woman, to touch her skin, to feel a connection—but that was false, just like everything about Lindsey Monahan.

He pulled out his phone and checked the clock. In fifteen minutes he would have to explain to Dean Cruz that the new addition to his team was a disaster. Words tumbled through his brain, none of them forming into any kind of explanation he wanted to give. He certainly couldn't explain that he and his new student almost...well, almost had the hottest sex he had had in years. Unbidden, he felt a stirring below his belly. The taste of her skin remained sweet on his tongue. He began to sink back into the luscious memory of the early evening when he heard a tinny voice.

"Professor, you're early."

Zach turned and saw Dean Cruz make her way up the steps, followed by a freshman carrying a stack of bags like a pack mule. She stopped a step below Zach and looked him up and down, her eyes lingering in all the wrong places.

"On the water again, I see?" she said. "My, you must have cultivated amazing endurance."

"Dean," Zach said, sweeping one arm toward the new administrative building. "After you."

"Door," she commanded the freshman. "Bags inside my office, if you will."

Zach threw a glance at the poor kid carrying her stuff. Those bags weighed more than he did. Zach darted ahead of him and opened the door. The freshman peeked out from behind the top package and grinned. "Thanks, dude."

Dean Cruz swept in through the open door, her perfume trailing behind her. Even on a Saturday, she wore a quarter inch of cosmetics and a tight fitting suit. He exhaled, trying to get the stench out of his nose before going in to strike a balance between keeping his self-respect and kissing her behind. *I can't believe this is my life,* he thought. *Remember, the greater good, Zach. Remember what The Delta Program could do for people.*

As they entered her office, the precariously carried bags toppled over and hit the floor with a thud. The dean squeezed her eyes shut, then peeled them open to glare at the freshman. "You may go," she said.

The freshman stood, looking somewhat stunned, his mouth gaping open.

"What?" she asked in exasperation.

"The class..." he blurted in a hurried cascade of words, "the class...you said I could audit...I need you to sign that form."

Dean Cruz looked flatly at the boy and exhaled deeply to make her displeasure clear. "Come back tomorrow. I'll see what I can do."

The boy had turned beet red by then and his shoulders had dropped into a defeated curve. He nodded and walked out, closing the door softly behind him.

"Finally," the dean said, pulling her chair out and pretending to tuck an already shellacked piece of hair behind one ear, "we are alone."

He nodded and shoved his hands into his pants pockets, then removed them just as quickly, feeling like he was about to be dressed down like that freshman.

Dean Cruz tapped her red lacquered nails together and stared at him with a look of regret on her face. A long, uncomfortable moment flew through the room. "When I first brought you into this school, I expected great things from you," she said. "Innovations, accolades."

He felt his brow stiffen again and tried to relax his face. "Actually, President Sanders brought me in, if you'll remember."

"True, but I approved your funding," she said. "And I still do."

"And I appreciate it."

"You do? Then where is my demo program?"

Zach paused. "We are close. We've made advancements three semesters in a row."

"Yes, but with no work product. The art programs produce art. The biology program, working samples, the architecture program just completed an entire building, for God's sake. How can I keep justifying throwing piles of cash at your very expensive program without something, *anything*, to show for it?"

"The Delta Program is...we are creating a

language no one has ever created before. It takes time. I…" He shifted in his chair. "I appreciate your continued faith in the project."

"Faith? Faith wasn't our deal. You promised results. Results. That was our deal."

Zach felt a muscle tighten in his chest. "We'll get there."

A small, patronizing whine escaped her. "That's what you said last year. What do you have to offer this semester?" she leaned forward, eyeing him directly. "Professor, I know you have worked hard, and no one can accuse you of not being ambitious, but let's just level with each other. You're stuck, right?"

"What? No," He said, re-crossing his legs as nonchalantly as he could. "We're not stuck, we just need a little more time."

Dean Cruz leaned back, and undid the top button of her blazer. "You ask a lot of me, Zach," she said, her eyes trailing down his torso. "And every time you do, I provide, do I not?"

Zach grimaced and felt his skin curdle. "You do."

"Like those new servers, and late admission for your new coder. I gave you those things, didn't I?"

Breath caught in his chest as his night with Lindsey came rushing back to his mind. He could almost feel the tenderness of her skin under the tips of his fingers. The longing and the betrayal swam side by side through his mind.

"I gave you those things, and now you need to give something to me," the dean continued. "I need a demo program by the end of this semester, or I'm pulling your funding."

Zach sat up. "What? What does that mean?"

"Funding for your lab will be gone. Zero. Nada," she said, making a cutting motion with her fingers.

"You can't be serious."

"Deadly serious. I've waited long enough."

"I know you expect—"

"Results," she said, cutting him off. "My God, this conversation is becoming redundant. You know how I hate that, Zach."

He opened his mouth, but she raised a hand. "And please, don't waste my time telling me for the tenth time that the technology you need doesn't exist. If it doesn't, create it. Am I clear?"

"You can't—"

"I can." She gave him a sad smile. "I don't want to, so please, don't force my hand."

He sat back, the room spinning. They were too close to fail now.

"I can see I've surprised you," she continued. "Which surprises *me*, honestly, because I thought you were more intuitive than that."

Zach's brain swam with loose code and algorithms that flew adrift, none of them connecting, none of them useful. He had five months to create his own Rosetta Stone to decode them and translate them into one master program. He only knew one coder that could do that—Lindsey Monahan.

His head fell into his hands. He remembered his final words to her, *"You're out. Don't you step a foot near my lab."* Regret flooded through him. Regret that he kicked her out, and at the vision of her wide brown eyes looking back at him sadly as he slammed her door and walked away.

She was the only coder he knew that could make his program work, but was it her code that he needed…or her?

Chapter 9: Lindsey

Lindsey pulled her legs into her body and curled up beneath her one unpacked blanket. A bright, horrible light was shining through the window, but she was unwilling to get up and close the blinds. "Screw you, daylight," she mumbled as she squeezed her eyes shut and pulled her head deeper below the covers. She willed Sunday to turn back to Saturday, when the morning light meant a new adventure. Now it meant loading everything she owned back onto a truck and admitting defeat.

A door opened and closed somewhere in the building. Lindsey jerked upright and looked at her front door. She prayed she would hear footsteps coming up the stairs followed by a knock, but nothing happened. Was he down there? She wiped her eyes then looked at the hardwood floor as if she could see him in the apartment below. Instead, she saw the bright green case of her cell phone buried in a pile of wadded-up tissue. She reached out and grabbed it. 9 am. She snapped the phone shut and listened again for any movement from below.

Maybe she could go down and knock on his door. Maybe if she just explained and fought for herself, she might convince him to change his mind. This was an epic misunderstanding, if only—no. She winced as she remembered his final, biting words: *you're out.* She felt what was once a vivid dream begin to slip from the edges of her vision as she buried herself again under the blanket. She opened her phone and hit the favorites button, where her mom's picture popped up in the first position.

Lindsey sniffed. Was it wrong to still need her mom? It had just been the two of them for a decade. The day after Lindsey left for college, her dad packed up and left. No wonder he encouraged her to matriculate so young; he wanted her to leave so he could do the same. Six months later, when Lindsey gave up and came home, she saw her mom, devastated and lonely, waiting with open arms to get through their dual heartbreaks together. Lindsey knew she would do the same now. They had each other, after all; that's all either one of them needed. The last two days flew by so quickly, she didn't think a lot about how her sudden departure would affect her mom. She must be so lonely.

Lindsey decided to hit dial and listened to the

phone begin to ring. Immediately, it clicked over to voice mail. "Hello, this is Pam. Please, leave a—" Lindsey hung up and wiped her eyes with the corner of her sleeve. She imagined her mom out working in the garden, as usual. Lindsey wished she was there, helping, or bringing out iced-tea. Worcester was only an hour away. She could be there before the sun went down.

Lindsey looked slowly around the stark corners of her apartment and sniffed. Everything was not lost. After all, her boxes were already packed. *That was one good thing, right?* She just had to rehire movers and head home. She liked her basement more than this stupid old building anyway.

Lindsey threw water on her face, brushed her teeth, and threw one essential bag over her shoulder. Her car was just five blocks away, and soon, she was maneuvering out of the city and on to I-90. As she did, she tried her mom again. No answer.

Lindsey wiped her nose and looked up. "Shoot!" she said, moving into the right lane. Her exit had passed in a blur. That's okay, she could hit the 395 at Auburn and circle back.

Twenty minutes later, her car pulled below the shady, giant tree that careened out of their suburban front lawn. She exhaled as she saw her mom's old Subaru parked in the driveway. This is where she belonged. After having a long talk, Lindsey wanted to curl up in the basement on her old, plaid couch, under her pictures of Einstein and Madonna and sleep until the pain was gone. She would go back to Boston for her stuff later, when she was sure Zach — or Professor Wheeler, wouldn't be around.

The front door swung open. "Mom?" Lindsey called out, dropping her bag in the foyer. "Mom?" She wasn't in the kitchen. Lindsey walked to the back door and looked out; she wasn't in the garden, either. In fact, there were holes in the chicken-wire where bunnies had gotten through and eaten the tops of the vegetables. That was strange.

Lindsey turned and heard a faint thumping noise emanating from the basement. She must be down there vacuuming with the music on or something, she guessed as she opened the basement door. As she did, the pounding of the music intensified and she could see a red light bouncing across the basement floor and up the steps toward her.

A frown crossed Lindsey's face. She grabbed the stair-rail and made her way down the steps. As she entered the basement, her mouth dropped open. Across the room, where her bed used to be, stood a stripper pole, and her mom was on it.

Pam's breasts were barely contained in the cups of a red, burlesque style corset, but she shook them happily as she spun around the pole, a trail of feathers flying in her wake. On the couch before her, Lindsey could see the back of a man's balding head bobbing with the music. "Yeah, baby," he yelled, twirling a single black nylon in the air like a lasso. Lindsey fell back against the wall with a thud.

"Lindsey? Lindsey, honey..." her mom said, unwrapping her leg from the pole. "Oh my God, honey, what are you doing here?"

Lindsey tried to swallow, but her mouth had gone dry. With some effort, she walked forward and spun around in a circle, stunned. "What am I doing? Mom...what are *you* doing?" Lindsey asked. "And where is all my stuff?" Not only was her bed gone, but so were her tables and posters. In their place was a new bar and stereo with a karaoke machine. The windows were covered in red gauze, and in the center of the old shag carpeting was a dance floor made of flashing, multi colored lights.

Her mom threw on a shawl and skipped over the dance floor to the clip of her stiletto heels. "This was all supposed to be a surprise. Surprise, honey!" Her mom splayed her fingers out in a pair of jazz hands, then dropped them as she read Lindsey's face. "Alright, busted. What can I say? You surprised me. I was going to tell you, I — wait..." her mom said, pulling a remote control out of her bust and muting the stereo. "What are you doing here, Lindsey? Is something wrong?"

All Lindsey could do was shake her head. If she spoke, she would cry.

The man on the couch took advantage of the silence. He popped up and walked over, wiping his hands on the sides of his boxer shorts along the way. He had more hair on his chest than on his head, and he wore nothing else but a pair of argyle socks pulled half way up his calves. "Hi there, Lindsey. Lindsey, right? Your mom's told me so much about you."

Lindsey looked down at his beefy, outstretched hand and sniffed.

"Hon," her mom sang gently, "this is Bruce."

Lindsey looked from her mom to the man. "Bruce?" It was all Lindsey could manage.

"So happy to meet you," he grinned, retracting his hand awkwardly and placing both hands on his hips. "Pam is so proud of you. You're all she's talked about for weeks."

"Weeks?"

Pam sighed. "Go sit down, Bruce," she said, "I'll be back soon." She took Lindsey by both arms and pulled her close into a long, forceful hug. Lindsey felt the scratch of the corset against her and tried to pull away, but Pam reeled her back in, pulling her close.

"Mom, seriously, this hug is way too long."

"Well, alright," Pam pulled away, but didn't let go of Lindsey's arms. "Let's get to it, then. What's going on? Are you okay?"

Lindsey frowned. "I...no. I'm not okay, Mom. Every thing's ruined and...and...," she wiped her eyes. "What happened to my basement?"

"Well, look," Pam shrugged. "You've moved on, honey, and so have I."

Lindsey looked around. She could barely remember what the basement looked like before. "But…it's only been two days."

"True, but…well, honey…I've been waiting a while."

Lindsey sniffed. "Whadya mean?"

"Well, sweetheart, when your dad left, you were my number one priority. And I love you, don't get me wrong, I just…it's time to do me."

"Do you?" Lindsey said, peering over her shoulder at Bruce, who waved at her from the sofa. "Ewww, Mom. Gross."

"Ha-ha," Pam said. "You listen now, you can do anything you want. You don't need to be stuck in some dingy basement with your mom forever. It's time. Whatever's happening, you go put on your big-girl panties and deal with it."

Lindsey looked down at the thong her mother wore. "Wow," she said flatly. "You're going to lecture me about panty size? That's funny."

"She's got you there, Pam!" Bruce called out from the sofa, uninvited.

Lindsey scanned the room. "I'm mortified, truly," she said, frowning. "And where did you even get all of this stuff?"

"Amazon!" yelled Bruce. "And Vicky's!" his eyes softened. "Isn't Pam a beauty?"

Lindsey watched as her mom's face bloomed into a smile. She bent her head and threw Bruce a wink. "You just wait, lover, I'll be with you in two shakes." To emphasize her words, she gyrated her hips.

"Woo-hoo!" yelled Bruce.

"Oh, my God," Lindsey pulled her hand over her face. "I'm in a nightmare. This is officially a nightmare."

Pam pulled Lindsey into another hug. "Listen, honey," she said gently in Lindsey's ear. "I'm not dead. And neither are you. Go live your life."

Panic surged through Lindsey like a wave of cold water. Go live her life? What life? Her dream of a college degree, and now, her only safe place in the world, were both gone. The emptiness of her options engulfed her. Her mom was talking but Lindsey couldn't understand the words. "Huh?" she muttered.

A buzzing rattled her spine. She didn't know if she should ask her mom if she'd lost a sex-toy, or take herself to the emergency room. The buzz radiated up one leg. As if from a distance, Lindsey realized it was her cell phone buzzing from inside her pocket. As she pulled it out, she saw a text from Zach Wheeler illuminating the screen.

"I expect you in the lab at 9am. The Project continues. Don't be late."

Lindsey blinked and read the text three more times. She felt a surge of electricity radiate through her chest. It felt like panic and lust, and something else. She mumbled something to her mom as she ran up the stairs and out to her car without stopping. She sped back toward Boston, and back toward Zach as fast as her car would take her.

Chapter 10: Zach

Zach turned the final lock on the server room door and made his way back into his office, his heart racing so fast he couldn't sit down. He looked down at his phone again. Had she received his text? He clenched the still dark screen in his fist and threw himself onto his bed to run through his strategy one more time. He had reconfigured the server. Changed all his passwords. All of everyone's passwords. He did a sensitive data transfer. He changed his personal security protocols. Even Lindsey couldn't get through...he hoped.

Pushing himself up onto one arm, he looked out across the lab. It was deserted, as usual, on a Sunday afternoon, and the stark, empty terminals bounced with screen savers, their choppy light creating patterns across the cold, linoleum floor. Far across the room blinked a single green light, expectantly waiting for Lindsey's arrival.

Zach frowned and jumped up, pushing up his already pushed up sleeves, then grabbed an empty cart and rolled it down to Lindsey's cube. His fingers plucked all of her equipment from its tethers and loaded it onto the cart in a pile, then pushed it all back toward his office. Just outside his window sat an empty cube. She had been set up there this morning, but earlier, he decided he wanted her as far from him as possible. But, on second thought, if she was closer, he could keep an eye on her. He wanted her close. Very, very close. And he knew he couldn't keep his eyes off of her, no matter where she was sitting.

As he plugged in her monitor, a pale blue light bathed the corners of the cube, reminding Zach of the soft sheen of Lindsey's pale skin in the moonlight. He imagined her sitting here, her brown eyes looking up at him, her skin glowing, her breasts bare like they had been in his hands and beneath the tender caress of his tongue. *'I can't believe this is happening'*, she had whispered. He looked out again at where she would be sitting Monday morning and felt his limbs tingle. *Shake it off, Wheeler*, he chided himself. *Focus. She can't be trusted.*

Zach got up and walked back to his own desk, forcing himself to focus on something else. He dialed his brother for the third time that day. The call went straight to voice mail, as usual. Zach tapped both hands against the desk, then swiped his mouse, lighting up his monitors. On one, he typed into the U.S. Marshall server and found Sam's system. It would be so easy to get the information he wanted. He tapped his fingers against the mouse and debated with himself. The end never justified the means. Hacking was tantamount to stealing, but, he needed information. And, if Sam had just picked up the phone, he would have done a data search for Zach anyway, right? Then breaking into his brother's database didn't really count as hacking...right?

Zach cursed at himself then plunged ahead. He created a duster to cover his trail and applied a decoding program to Sam's system. The screen began to whir as firewalls dropped and his brother's password was decoded. On a second screen, he pulled up the university's current donor list, and on a third monitor, pictures of the President's Tea he'd found in the school's on-line paper. He circled the faces of the donors and compared them to the guests. None of them matched. If he could just find out who these new donors were and who they were working for, he'd feel a lot better about the dean's sudden demand for a demo program.

His system blinked as the activity on monitor one spun to a stop. *Access Denied*, a pop-up read. He tried again. *Access Denied: network alert: port scan attack is logged.*

His teeth ground together. "Dammit, Sam," he

said, shaking his head. "I thought you never listened to me." Zach recognized the alert; he had created the program that delivered it. Sam had finally gotten around to protecting his system. Zach could dig more, undo the program with a virus and install a trojan, but that really would be hacking. He hit *shut down all* and watched as all his monitors popped and went black.

In the sudden darkness of his office, he looked down at his phone. Still no response from Lindsey. He listened in the shadows at the distant chirping of his servers, drumming unevenly like the beating of his heart. He looked out again at her empty cube. Tomorrow he would be faced with her, all of his attraction and fear pooling into the small space between their two desks.

To assuage his anxiety, he hit a button and his office was awash with light as all his monitors lit up, then filled with social media sites of all kinds. On one keyboard he entered code, then /LindseyMonahan/ then search. Still nothing. Lindsey had absolutely no social media presence. There were no pictures, no feeds, no blogs, no tweets, no posts, no info. She was a ghost, just like him.

He tapped at a desktop file and opened her university application for the tenth time. She had filled out only the required fields, nothing more. Scrolling down to the very bottom of the last page, he saw one piece of information he had never noticed before. There was one name listed under references: Kate Piper. His heart leaped.

Zach opened up his social media program again and searched for Kate Piper. Multiple files jumped forward, arranged in tiles that ran across all five screens. Kate Piper: PR expert, Crisis Manager and Partner at KinCo Industries. Zach typed 'show images', and a slew of photos flooded the screen. A dazzling brunette smiled from the pictures, many next to a handsome man. She was dipping in his arms, he was pushing back a tendril of her hair, adoringly. Then, in the background of one, Zach found what he was looking for. There, her small frame almost hidden in a crowd, was Lindsey. He cut around her, cropped the image and enlarged it. Even through the distortion of the pixels her eyes and perfect heart-shaped face seemed to look directly at him. A smile lingered on her lips as if she had just been laughing, or as if she was going to whisper through the photo and tell him something. He drew in a breath. He hadn't imagined it—she was as beautiful as he remembered.

Zach reached out to touch her face, then snapped his hand back. "Don't be a fool," he told himself out loud. "Separate. You need her talent. You don't need her." He squeezed his eyes shut and fell back in the chair, the words *I do need her* running like a contrary loop through his mind.

His phone suddenly vibrated and jumped across the surface of his desk. He lunged forward and snatched it up.

"I'll be there," read a text from Lindsey.

Zach's heart raced as he read the text again, when another popped up. *"And I'm sorry,"* it read.

Zach clenched the phone and looked again at her photo. Maybe she was just a wonderful girl he met in a bar—she just happened to be one of the world's best coders. *The two things didn't have to be mutually exclusive, right?* He felt all the muscles in his body tense in hope that that was true, but then felt something snap deep in his chest. He had just put his life's work at risk by inviting a world-class hacker into his sanctuary. He prayed this wasn't a mistake, then swallowed hard and willed himself to bury his desire.

Chapter 11: Lindsey

Students zoomed passed Lindsey as she stepped to the side to check her map, once again. She frowned as the direction went vertical and then horizontal, then landed definitively with a street view and a pin. *One minute to your destination*, it read. Her mouth went dry as her eyes followed the curving path ahead, over the yellowing of the trees and into the sky above where she saw the looming stone turrets of building 313. This was it.

As the trees cleared she saw two giant wooden doors above a wide, deep set of stairs, on which students lounged happily in the sun. She maneuvered through the bodies and up the steps toward the entrance, trying to calm the pulse ringing in her ears. As she stepped into the cool air of the foyer, she found a black directory that hung against the far wall. She read it, then turned right, where the golden wooden corridor gave way to a stark, industrial hallway. At the end, hidden over an adjacent door, was a small sign that read "Data Science Lab."

"You can do this, Lindsey, you can do this." She chanted to herself. "Your diploma is on the other side. *Zach* is on the other side." She gripped the cold handle of the door. "You can do this," she told herself again, and with a final deep breath, pushed the door open.

The door closed behind her with a soft whoosh of air. As her eyes adjusted to the dim light within, she saw three guys standing around a workstation, one blond with a popped up collar, and two others straight out of dork-central casting. Lindsey leaned forward to see what they were working on. The screen was filled with the photo of a pretty girl who looked to be a student. "Watch this," the blond said, then hit the enter button on the keyboard. In a flash, the girl's face turned into a mule that brayed over and over on a loop, its toothy face swinging forward and back.

"Nice!" said one of the dorks. "Hey, can you do a gorilla? I know this other chick that would be perfect as a gorilla."

Lindsey heard a heavy sigh from the corner. She turned to see a dark, lanky man at another terminal leaned back in his chair, a pair of impossibly high gold stiletto boots swung over the desk in front of him. He was filing his nails, and above his eyes were two perfect eyebrows adorned with arches of gold sequins. Lindsey wondered absently how he glued them on. "Imbeciles," he murmured.

Lindsey held tight to her bag as she scanned the far corners of the lab, Zach was nowhere to be seen. She stepped in closer and cleared her throat. "Excuse me," she ventured softly.

The blond looked up quickly, then back to his screen. "Just put the pizza down," he said.

Lindsey frowned. "Pizza? Oh, gosh no. I'm not...I'm here to meet Professor Wheeler."

The blond turned his smug face toward her and scanned her arms. "If you don't have pizza, what good are you? Get out, and don't come back unless you have pizza." One dork let out a sudden snort followed by a laugh. All three turned to look at her with giant, goofy smiles plastered across their faces.

Anxiety began to swirl in Lindsey's belly. *You're older now,* she told herself. *You're a woman. Don't let them get you down this time.* She squared her shoulders to say something back when she heard the door open behind her, followed by a rush of cool air being pulled out of the room. She turned to find Zach, looming silently behind her. Relief flooded over her at the sight of him, and she had the urge to throw her arms around his neck, but his jaw was clenched as he gazed at her, his eyes the same suspicious ones she saw the other night. "I..." she stammered, her weight falling onto one hip. "Hi."

Zach's smoldering stare washed over her before

his jaw tightened and he breezed past her into the lab without a word. A tremor of disappointment surged through her as she watched him turn toward the team and cross his arms. As he did, Lindsey drank in his features. He was as tall and bronze as she remembered, and even in the cool light from the monitors, she found him inexplicably handsome. His features were large, but were all delicately molded into a perfect dream of a face that now turned toward her coldly as he began to speak. "Team," he said, "heads up." All faces swiveled toward him, then toward Lindsey, seeing the glare in his eyes. "This is Viper."

Lindsey's skin went cold. "Lindsey," she muttered. "My name is Lindsey."

The blond student with the popped up collar let his mouth fall open. "No way," he said, staring. "No *F-ing* way."

"Well, how about that!" The man with the sequined eyebrows said, spinning in his chair. "This *is* going to be a fun day."

The blond shook his head dramatically, looking toward the two dorks for approval before continuing. "Hold up, Professor. I'm feeling a total disconnect. Minnie Mouse here is Viper?"

Zach nodded and stared at Lindsey as he answered, his cautious eyes skimming over her. "Don't let the exterior fool you, James." He glared. "She's the one."

James walked over next to Zach and crossed his

arms, mirroring the Professor's body as he snickered. "You hacked into our game?" he asked Lindsey. "The un-hackable game none of us could get into?" He shook his head until a long blond lock fell effortlessly over one eye. "Impossible."

Lindsey's eyes darted across the new faces then back at Zach. He stared silently. "It was a pretty surface level environment," Lindsey offered. "I found backdoors, I—"

"No." James interrupted, shaking his hair from his eye. "We designed that game so communication was wired inside of the firmware. Impossible."

Zach stared at Lindsey. She couldn't tell if she saw admiration or disgust in his eyes. "It was impossible to us," he said. "It wasn't for her."

Lindsey felt an opening. "Ask me anything," she blurted toward Zach. "Anything. I'm...not that complicated." Zach's biceps clenched beneath the fabric of his shirt, but he did not respond, so Lindsey continued. "I just...I found Zach's—Professor Wheeler's—IP and joined using his own channel. That's when I decided to hack all the traffic on your network and piece it together backwards. It just...it made sense."

"Bullshit!" yelled James, turning toward Zach with a raised hand. "I call bullshit."

The sequined-man in the corner slapped down his nail file, hoisted himself up effortlessly on his stilettos and glided over. "Stuff it, James," he said in passing, then turned toward Lindsey. He stood about a foot above her and looked down at her with a wry smile on his shiny lips. "Impressive," he said, offering his hand. "I say Kudos. I'm Cedric, by the way."

"Um, thanks, Cedric." Lindsey smiled, feeling her anxiety wane. "You tried to make your server anonymous, but nothing's anonymous, really, not anymore." She looked up and her eyes locked onto Zach's.

"Don't spoon feed them all the answers, Ms. Monahan. They can figure it out on their own time." As Zach continued to stare at her, her skin grew hot and she realized she didn't exhale until he turned back toward the team. "Lindsey will be joining us as Team Lead, along with Cedric and James."

"Is this a joke?" James blurted. "Team Lead? She just got here."

"Bury the ego, James," Zach said. "Our latest model is no good and Ms. Monahan—"

"Lindsey," she blurted.

"Lindsey," he continued with a nod, "should be an asset."

James guffawed then plopped like a spoiled child into his chair. "What's the big deal?" he said. "We all have enough credits to graduate already. At least I do. Who cares about some stupid prototype program? It was just an experiment, anyway."

Lindsey watched as disbelief flashed across Zach's face. He twisted his neck slightly and took a measured breath before speaking. "I know in five years you want to be on a yacht in Cabo, James, but you have a chance to be on the right side of history here, to do something good with your life."

"My life is good now, bro. Besides, I have plenty of interest in my own algorithm."

"Here we go again..." Cedric murmured.

Zach re-crossed his arms. "Right," he said. "The famous algorithm. Remind me...that's the one that makes people buy more stuff?"

"It's called elasticity modeling. What's wrong with that?"

"Nothing..." Zach shrugged. "But the work we do here will change the whole world. It will effect real people, and real things, like health care, infrastructure, food supply." Zach paused, but James only replied with a smug stare. Zach closed his eyes briefly, then opened his arms wide to the group. "Listen, everyone, this code, *our code*, will make cities responsive organisms. Like a body releasing antibodies to heal an injury, our code can be used to heal entire communities."

Lindsey watched as passion radiated from Zach's eyes and mouth. To Lindsey, he looked suddenly a foot taller. His words made something click deep inside her mind. Code for the greater good. She had never even considered that.

As Zach continued, she buried the desire to run and kiss him. Or run to her computer to build this code that he needed. Or both. *Please, God,* she thought to herself, *let it be both.* As a throbbing began to grow in her chest, she pulled out her phone. She had to talk to him—to set everything right. Quietly, she texted Zach: *Can we talk?* She was just about to press send, when Zach continued.

"Listen. You've all heard me say it before, but words are cheap. Tonight, I want each of you to go home and ask yourself: are you here to contribute something?" His eyes blazed. "If you are, be here first thing tomorrow, prepared to work."

Words are cheap, he'd said. Lindsey's hand froze. She quickly tucked her phone under her arm and erased the text with her thumb.

The group dispersed slowly, leaving Zach and Lindsey to stare at each other in silence across the lab. With some effort, she watched Zach pick up his bag and walk toward her. He leaned in and spoke quietly. "Do we need to talk?"

Lindsey steadied herself with a breath, even as her heart surged. He was so close she could smell the briny, warm scent rising from his skin. "Nope," she said, trying not to lean forward and plant her lips on his jaw. "And I don't need to think about it. I'm in."

Zach leaned back and looked at her quizzically, doubt or disappointment flashing in his eyes. His jaw tightened as he took two steps back. "Okay, Viper. I'll email you the files you need. Get up to speed," he said, "and fast."

Chapter 12: Zach

Zach twisted his blinds open an inch and scanned the hunched figures that peppered the lab. Electricity surged through the room as he listened to the rhythmic, tapping fingers of his coders. There was a tangible change in the air since Lindsey was planted at the head of the room, like a Viking masthead carved to the front of a ship, she paved the way through new waters.

She arrived early each morning before everyone except him. He watched from his office as she embedded herself in her cube without a word, an eager gleam to her eye as she waited for her monitors to blink to life. But, unlike everyone, within moments, she was leaned back in her chair, her limbs loose, her head tilted in thought. She was biting her lip and tapping signals onto her leg with the tips of her fingers. Zach recognized the pattern.

She was typing rows of invisible numbers, zeros and ones, over and over, her hands a conduit for the code that flew through her brain, so fast she had to let it seep out her fingers.

She leaned forward and raised her delicate fingers to her keyboard and began to type. As she did, Zach watched the light of the lab envelop the soft skin of her neck in pale blue light. He longed to walk out and decorate that neck with kisses. Instead, he silently willed her almond eyes to turn and look at him. They did not, and had not since she had begun her work last week.

Each day, brilliant new code flooded into his inbox, but she did not speak to him. He should be thrilled, but only felt a simmering disappointment burnish the edges of his excitement. He let the blinds slap shut and pulled his long arms up and over his head, hoping blood would begin to flow into other parts of his body besides his groin. No matter how much rowing he did, or how much he tried to think of other things, his body seemed to only be focused on Lindsey — on her skin, her mind, and her laugh. As each silent day passed, he found his longing grow and his ability to dismiss it weaken.

He had secretly hoped to catch her in the hallway of their building, but her windows were always dark. This morning, before dawn, he looked up to see no light shining from within. He raced to the lab, thinking she might be there, but her cubicle sat dark and untouched. He dropped his head and rubbed the back of his neck roughly with his palm. *Where did she go every day?*

A clickety-clack rang across the floor outside his office, followed by a knock that vibrated through his metal office door. Zach straightened up and combed his fingers through his hair. "Yeah," he called out expectantly.

Cedric pushed the door open and stuck his face in. Zach scanned today's costume. Cedric wore faded jeans and a tank top, but over that, a pale blue kimono was draped over his reedy, black shoulders. He had two chopsticks stuck in a bun atop his head and on his feet were wooden, Japanese sandals.

Cedric grinned and leaned against the door jamb. "Shame on you, Professor."

Zach stiffened. *Had Cedric seen him staring?* "I'm not in the mood for jokes."

"Oh, no jokes this time. You're trouble, and, apparently, I'm not the only one that's figured that out."

"Uh huh." Zach said flatly. "I'll bite. What are you talking about?"

Cedric slid into Zach's office, his face flushed. "Well, don't give yourself away by acting guilty, but there is a devastatingly handsome U.S. Marshall outside this very door.

Zach blinked once then buried his face in his palm. "Oh, God."

"Oh, *yes.*"

Zach groaned and leaned around Cedric to see into the darkness of the lab. "Okay." he said glumly. "Let him in."

Cedric glided back toward the door, turned, then flipped the tail of his kimono back with a snap. "Listen, boss, I'm always good for a jail break if you need me."

"Just let him in."

"Alright. But remember what Buddha said, 'Chaos is inherent in all things. Strive on with diligence'."

"Seriously, Cedric. Not today."

"Jeez, well, alright then." Cedric opened the door wide to reveal Zach's brother, Sam, his giant frame dominating the doorway. "He says you can come in now, Sam, but don't be too hard on him."

Sam looked down at Cedric, who was almost his height. "Thanks, Cedric. Stay out of trouble."

"Come on, now," Cedric said, sailing past him and into the lab. "You know me better than that."

"I do," Sam said as he entered the doorway. "That's why I said it."

Sam shut the door behind him and glared down at Zach. His two crossed arms looked like tree trunks stuffed into his suit jacket as he spoke. "Hacking into a government database is a federal offense."

Zach shrugged. "You wouldn't return my calls."

"I should arrest you."

"Sure. But who would help you next time you

accidentally erased a file? Besides, if you would answer your phone, you would have helped me."

"Would not."

"You would too. You always do."

Sam uncrossed his arms and shrugged. "I couldn't answer. I was on a case."

Zach scanned his brother's face. He knew that look from when they were kids, when Sam was always trying to talk his way out of trouble. "I thought that case was over."

"Okay," Sam said, twisting his mouth. "Guilty. I had to turn off my personal cell phone for a few days."

"I knew it. Let me guess, another girl problem?"

Sam grinned. "Hey, the ladies love me."

"Right." Zach said. "*All* of them."

"What can I say? I didn't mean to be the *only* brother born with devastating good looks, but shit happens."

"Your ego is unbelievable. Truly."

"To be fair, I guess you do have *some* appealing qualities. If you ever pulled your head out of your books, you could do something with them."

"I've got better things to do than chase tail."

"See?" Sam's smile widened, revealing two deep dimples. "You make my point. I have to make up for your embarrassing lack of prowess. You know, save the family name."

Zach exhaled. "Shouldn't we get back to you chastising me? I'd rather be arrested than listen to more of this."

"Alright," Sam said, leaning back. "What gives? What was so important you had to break in?"

Before Zach could answer, another knock rang against the door.

"Yeah?" Zach called out. The door pushed open and Lindsey's heart-shaped face peeked inside.

Zach straightened his back. Before he could get out a word, Sam stepped forward.

"Hi there, honey," he said. "What's your name?"

Zach stood. "Back off, Sam."

"What? I'm sure this young lady would like to get to know the more charming Wheeler brother."

"I—" Lindsey said, then shut her mouth, her head darting back and forth between Zach and Sam. "Is this a bad time? I can come back…"

Sam shot Lindsey a practiced, charming smile. "Not for me. This is the perfect time."

"Sam…" Zach growled. "Seriously."

Sam's eyebrows raised and he pressed his fist against his upturned lips. "Sorry, bro," he said. "I didn't know you got yourself a girl."

"She's not—"

Sam slugged him in the shoulder. "It's about time, player."

"Please. Please, just arrest me," Zach pleaded.

Sam raised his considerable arms up in a sign of surrender and leaned back against the wall, a baffled smile on his face.

Zach turned his tense body toward the door. "Sorry, Lindsey. Come in."

Zach could see a pink flush bloom across her cheeks as she stepped inside the room.

"Um..." she said. "Did you get my latest?"

"Yup. Looks good," Zach answered, trying to relax his back. "Good work. Really good."

"Good?" Lindsey's face fell.

"Yup," Zach said with a nod. "Were you just checking in, or...?"

Lindsey teetered on one heel, her frown deepening. "Yes," she said. "I mean, no." She shook her head. "I...I have to tell you something."

Zach felt his muscles tense. "Alright."

Lindsey swallowed. "I was creating a bridge between two of your core programs. The code works, but," she said as she jammed her hands into her pockets, "it looks like someone bleached part of the data."

Zach surged forward a foot then stopped abruptly. "Are you sure?"

"Yeah. It's shredded, but I think I can put it back together. It will just take time."

"Which file?"

"I was in the main frame when I found it. I'll send you a link. I can install a trip wire so it won't happen again," she offered.

"No," Zach blurted.

"Why not? It's easy. Don't you want to—"

"No," Zach snapped. "And don't touch the

main frame. I'll send you the sections one by one from now on."

Lindsey's color drained from red to white as she nodded, a deep sorrow dragging at the corners of her eyes. She reached silently for the door and did not look back as the door shut with a click behind her. Zach felt his hand reach out to stop her, but no words would come.

"Wow, Zach. How do you do it?" Sam asked.

"I—" Zach swallowed. "She's a hacker. I have to be careful."

Sam crossed his arms smugly. "No. I mean, how can you get anything done with that girl in the next room?"

Zach rubbed his eyes, knowing his brother could see right through him. "It was a mistake."

"She sure doesn't look like a mistake."

"Looks can be deceiving," Zach said, anguish flashing across his face.

"Okay, bro," Sam said, throwing up his hands. "I'll let you wallow in whatever mess you think you've made here, but remember, life is short. Have fun," Sam said, his face suddenly tense. "I'm serious. If you don't live while you can, you lose. Trust me."

"What," Zach asked, "and stick my hand in the fire? Even though I know I'll get burned?"

"Get burned, it's not so bad."

"That's easy for you to say. You don't stay with anyone long enough to get burned."

A heavy silence swung between them. "Wow." Sam hung his head. "Wow, Zach."

Zach squeezed his eyes shut, immediately regretting his words. "Sorry, Sam, I wasn't thinking, I—"

"No worries, brother," Sam said. "That was a long time ago."

"I guess…I just—like you said, my head is stuck in a book. It makes me an idiot sometimes."

"Understood, little brother. But give yourself a break. I can see your brain is spinning round and round like there's a gerbil on a wheel in there."

"Just like you when you get stuck on a case."

"True. But your gerbil is on 'roids. I don't even think your gerbil fits inside the wheel anymore. Like I said, live a little. Like, get with that girl out there."

Zach studied his brother's face. How he envied him, all his worries just sliding effortlessly away. "You live enough for both of us, Sam."

"Give it a rest sometimes. That's all I'm saying. And, hey, while I'm giving advice, here's some more: don't hack me."

"Yeah," Zach said, nodding. "Sorry about that."

Sam looked at his brother evenly. "Tell me, what was so important you almost broke your famous ethical standards?"

Zach shrugged. "My gut. There have been a lot of suits around and I don't know why."

"So? Schmoozers, right? Who cares?"

"Maybe. But I'm going to dig some more."

"You're not at war, Zach."

"You save the world in your way, I'll save it in mine."

"Understood, little brother," Sam said, as he walked toward the door. "My advice, follow the money. And hey, you know you can ask me about anything. Just don't forget about the asking part next time."

"Got it," Zach said. "Thanks."

"Catch you later," Sam said, pulling Zach into an embrace. "And don't lose out on that girl out there. She looks like a good one."

Zach felt a pang as he saw Lindsey sitting in her chair with her back turned. "We'll see..." he whispered.

Chapter 13: Lindsey

The sidewalks of campus were almost empty on Sunday, just the way Lindsey liked it. Her feet crunched across the browning leaves that had dried and dropped along the cobblestone path leading toward the lab, leaving the trees barren enough to reveal a graying sky. A sudden chilly breeze hit her bare neck and she pulled her collar up and frowned. She scurried up the now familiar stone steps toward the lab, suddenly aware that summer had gone too quickly and she had missed it, huddled in the lab trying to impress Zach into trusting her. Instead, he stared at her silently with his sexy, but perpetually skeptical, eyes, watching her every move.

Today's agenda scrolled through her mind as she entered the building. She had made progress this week and thought perhaps she could bridge the latest set of code and have it in his inbox by morning. Maybe that would show him her intentions were good. Of course, she thought that last week, and the week before, and instead of healing their rift, she felt a deepening chasm grow between them, separated only by the thin glass of his office window. To Lindsey, it felt like a sea between them, dark and vibrating with electricity.

The door to the lab opened with an unfamiliar click. Across the room, a projector came to life, sending pink bubbles of light into every corner, a virtual disco ball twirling across the room. A beat began, and suddenly, Donna Summer's voice filled the room, singing "Ooh, Love to Love You Baby." Lindsey felt her mouth drop open.

"I knew you'd be here, darling," Cedric's voice called out.

Lindsey turned to see him at his desk, his legs crossed demurely below a burgundy wrap dress which glowed red beneath the twirling disco lights. "Um..." was all she could manage.

"Come, come," Cedric said, turning an open briefcase toward her. Inside the case was a perfect 1960's traveling martini set, from which Cedric pulled a shaker and bottle. "How dirty do you like it?"

Lindsey felt a smile pull across her lips. "Pretty dirty," she answered.

"Ha!" Cedric laughed, pouring olive brine into the shaker. "I knew it." Deftly, he dropped in the ice and vodka and shook the concoction before straining the unctuous liquid into a tiny martini glass. He handed it to Lindsey and smiled, the lights bouncing across a subtle highlight of glitter decorating just the edge of his cheekbones. He leaned back and looked Lindsey up and down for dramatic effect. "I know what you're thinking," he said. "You wonder how someone as fabulous and busy as me has time for all this," he said, waving his arm in the air like a spokesmodel. "But I see you, and you could use a party, girl."

Lindsey wondered briefly if she should be offended, then decided he was right. She shrugged. "I do enjoy a good party."

"I knew you would. Now, sit with me," he said, rolling a chair up next to his own. "Let's talk. So..." he began. "Go. What's your story?"

Lindsey shook her head as she answered. "Not much to tell," she said, sitting down. "I'm super boring."

"What!" Cedric responded. "No girl, uh-uh. Not with me."

Lindsey gripped her hands together and looked at him wide eyed.

"Look." Cedric continued. "You, darling, are a prodigy. Close your mouth, where did you think you were? I did some digging, just like I'm sure you did about me."

"Okay," Lindsey admitted. "Maybe a little."

"Right. And I'm sure you found that Cedric has a past, dabbled a bit in some not so ethical behavior, *in my youth, understand*. I was just finding my way. And now I know — on a computer, Cedric is God."

"Wow, that's...bold."

"All those delicious little zeros and ones can create universes upon universes, and I am their creator."

"I guess."

"You guess? You must feel that way too... Viper."

Lindsey took a sip of her martini. "Nah, I think I'm just persistent."

"You? Come now, give yourself credit. You're bad-ass, but only you can figure that out for yourself. Like Buddha says, *'you alone must walk the path, girl.'*"

"Buddha, huh?"

"Oh, yes. I used to be a bit of a delinquent. But, if I hadn't walked my path, I would never be here. Know what I mean?"

"I guess." She frowned. "I mean...scratch that. Please, explain."

Cedric almost bounced in his chair as he sat forward. "Well," he said. "It's a tragic, but beautiful story. As a young pup, I stole cell phones for quick cash. Then, one day, I realized the data inside the phone was worth way more money. I know, *I know*, please don't judge. From there, I figured out how to plant Malware in people's devices and rob them blind. That's how Sam found me."

"Zach's brother?"

"Yes, and instead of sending me up the river for all time, he recommended community service in Zach's last lab. Now, here I am, reaching my full and glorious potential."

"Wow."

"Now, see? That was my path."

Lindsey took another sip of her martini and felt her head begin to spin. "I get it."

"Now, I try to even the scales, do good where I can. Like Professor Wheeler...or *Zach*, as you call him."

Lindsey flushed. "Just, Professor Wheeler seems so formal..."

"So, what have you learned about hunky Professor Zach?" Cedric asked, leaning back and swirling his drink.

"Nothing, really. No poking around. *No, no.* He hates that." She finished her drink. "Clearly."

"Impressive," Cedric said, grabbing the martini shaker and pouring Lindsey a second glass. "You have self-control. I would have been all up in the web if I liked him."

Lindsey almost spit out her latest sip. "What? No..."

"Don't look so surprised, honey, I'm a blood hound. I can smell pheromones." He pulled an olive out of his glass and popped it in his mouth. "I knew you two had already done a little slap and tickle the minute you walked in the door."

"Oh, God," Lindsey said, dropping her head.

"Your secret's safe with me, darling, and I doubt anyone else knows. Most of these people can't see past their monitors. So," he asked, "what do you want to know?"

"About Zach?"

"Sure. I'll lay out the basics. Raised by military parents, his brother followed that route, but Zach, after a rough youth, not unlike my own, decided education was key. He decided he could make a bigger impact through academics. Harvard, Stanford, MIT."

"Wow."

"Yes, and he carries the weight of the world on those luscious shoulders. He doesn't have to, but he just can't help himself."

"How so?" Lindsey asked.

"He feels called, girl. He wants to save the world and he wants to do that with code. He thinks he weighed the scales in the wrong direction enough in his youth. Now he works to push them the other way."

Lindsey remembered how he reacted to the idea she had hacked him, and how passionate he was when he described the Delta Project that first day. She felt a sliver of light begin to open as she downed her second martini. "And...single?"

Cedric grinned. "Yes, never married. Although, people try. Everyone takes their shot. Take the dean, for example."

"Dean Cruz? I haven't met her."

"Yes, freaky bitch. She's had so many injectables put in her face, she's starting to look like a melted candle."

"Ooh. That's harsh."

"I guess. But she's sketchy. I think she's a swinger."

"You hacked her too?"

Cedric grinned. "Don't tell."

Lindsey made a twisty motion of a lock and key at her lips, then took another sip.

"I knew we'd be friends," Cedric said, reaching for his laptop. "Like, take a look at this."

A screen popped up with a series of code, followed by a digital conversation.

"Look here," Cedric pointed at the text. 'I need Elysian Fields in four months.' Weird, right? Who needs Elysian Fields? That must be cipher for something. Every month she gets a new one, like a countdown clock. I need Elysian Fields in six months, then five. And that's just the beginning."

"Crazy. Who sent it?"

"Some lady named Brenda True. But I knew that couldn't be a real name, unless the dean is friends with a porn star."

"Based on what you've said, that might not be a stretch."

"Valid, I couldn't find anyone named Brenda True. I'm stuck, I guess," Cedric said, spinning in his chair, his laptop open like a carrot on a stick. "Maybe we'll never know."

Lindsey felt her skin flushing. "Send it to me," she said. "I'll see what I can find."

"Okay, girl. Hack on," Cedric said as he hit a button. "It's already in your box. Now, you go. What's your story? How'd you end up here?"

Lindsey felt her mind sink back. "Well, I started off fine. Great in fact. Then…then I got scared and ended up tethered to my computer in my mom's basement for a decade."

"Yikes."

"Yeah. I guess I was just stuck and time flew by."

"Well, good for you! You got unstuck. Coming here must have been a big decision."

Lindsey shrugged. "Big decisions are easy when there aren't any other options."

"What's this?" A voice sounded out, startling them both. Lindsey and Cedric looked up to see James scowling at the lights bouncing across the walls.

"This?" Cedric said. "This is dirty martinis and disco, James. This is what happens when Cedric makes a friend."

James stepped forward with a crooked frown. "Alcohol on campus is against university policy, Cedric."

Cedric exhaled loudly. "And this," he said, pointing at James, "this is James. This is what happens when humans are sexually frustrated."

"Fine," James quipped, "get expelled. Like I

care."

"Ooh," Cedric said, "that is so unfair, we were just going to invite you to join us."

James hesitated a second before responding. "Ha ha, Cedric. You degenerate."

"What's that? Oh, sorry, these beautiful ears can't hear jealousy."

"I'm not jealous, freak. I do just fine. Great in fact."

"Tell us all about it, James."

"Screw you," James said, walking back toward the door. "When I sell my algorithm you'll be working for me. You all will," he said, and walked out.

"What was that all about?" asked Lindsey.

"Oh, he's obsessed with the idea that he's going to sell his silly algorithm and retire by thirty."

Lindsey shrugged. "Maybe he will. Who knows, right?"

"True. Like us, James needs to walk his own path. His own douchey, douchey path."

Lindsey thought again about Cedric's words. Maybe this *was* her path. Maybe it was a curving, frustrating, wonderful path taking her where she needed to go. Maybe that path would still lead her toward her degree…and toward Zach. She thought about the days and weeks to come and about his smoldering eyes staring out at her from his office window. A sudden laugh burst from her lips.

"What's funny?" asked Cedric.

Lindsey shook her head with a quiet smile as Kate's words swam through her mind. *I'm Lindsey freaking Monahan*, she thought. "Nothing. Thanks for the drink. Now, I need to get to work."

Chapter 14: Zach

Zach hunched down behind his steering wheel as the door to his building swung open and Lindsey appeared carrying a bicycle under one arm. She stopped at the sidewalk to wrap a red scarf around her neck and pull her second arm through the strap of her backpack before swinging one long leg over the seat. He watched as she lifted the bike onto the pavement and looked hopefully down the street, a wisp of breath escaping her lips as she glided away in the cold morning air.

Pastel rays of morning light streamed around her lean body as she rolled gently down the street. Then, as the morning sun shot through two buildings and enveloped her, she stood up in the pedals and accelerated into a turn. Zach sat up in his seat, just in time to see golden light wash across her beautiful face, revealing a perfect curve on her lips. He was suddenly acutely aware that while she was smiling, he was frowning.

He jammed his key into the ignition and let his engine rumble to life as he wiped dew off of the inside of his windshield with his sleeve. As he pulled out behind her, he realized she must have ditched her car in exchange for the more nimble bicycle. He felt suddenly silly for looking out his apartment window every time an engine sparked to life on the street below. He wondered what else he had missed in the past weeks as the sterile silence between them grew.

Before Lindsey, he hadn't noticed any noise from the apartment above his. Now he found himself lying alone in his bed, holding his breath so he could hear the faint sounds of Lindsey walking along the floor above, hoping he would only hear one set of feet, and no intense voices like the ones they had the night they met. Every morning, he held his breath to hear her faint steps pad down the staircase outside his door and leave the apartment, only to rush to the lab and find it empty. But this morning, when he heard the water from her shower trickle through the pipes just after five am, he lurched out of bed and down to his car, determined to find out where she went in the barely light hours before she got to the lab.

As his car coasted down the street behind her, he blew into his fists to warm them, then slapped shut the laptop propped open beside him on the cold leather seat. Inside were cascades of files Lindsey had been sending him, each one more intricate and perfect than the last. Her code was exquisite, and as he read it, he felt himself falling headlong into the graceful curves of her work, the numbers forming a bridge that closed the divide between all other disparate programs. As he read them, he imagined her slender fingers working out the numbers like a symphony pianist, the vibration of her creativity making his own body quiver. Part of him longed to run to her, to kiss those fingers and talk to her about the work she was creating. The other part of him felt his doubt growing.

How could anybody be this good? This fast? How was she able to create waves and oceans of perfect code? She was either the best coder he had ever known, or someone else was feeding her the work. Perhaps the files were corrupted, a decoy designed to get into his server. Maybe she would collect it all and sell it. Or...maybe he was just being an idiot. As he pulled around the corner at the end of the street, he caught a glimpse of her a full block ahead. He accelerated, his eyes glued to her back wheel.

Way to go, stalker, he told himself. *Is this weird? If you have to ask yourself, the answer is yes. Turn away.* With a firm shake of his head and a wave of regret, he gripped the steering wheel to turn right as Lindsey turned left, but then, she went up onto a nearby sidewalk with a tiny thud and peddled across an open field.

His car lurched to a stop. She was heading in the direction of Harvard Yard. He scowled and took a sudden left, cutting off an oncoming car. The driver honked and flipped him off. Zach automatically ducked low in case the noise drew her attention, then accelerated through a yellow light ahead and flew through the winding streets of the Harvard Campus. His head turned in all directions, sorting through all the students meandering through campus on bicycles, when he saw Lindsey's undeniable frame pulling her bicycle into the parking lot of a coffee shop already packed with students.

Zach waited for a car to pull out, then shot blindly into the open space as possibilities raced through his mind. *Why would she be here? Was Harvard trying to steal her? Or MIT? Or was she selling the code? Or buying it?* He imagined her walking into the shop like a secret agent, dropping her backpack and picking up another without anyone seeing, putting on dark glasses and walking out. Is this what she did every day? Is this how she got the code?

He turned off his car and reached for the door. If he hurried, he could see who she was meeting. He would confront them and demand to know what was going on. Just then, he saw her squeeze back out through the coffee shop door, a coffee holder with two cups perched in one hand, a small paper bag hanging from the other. She walked to her bicycle and put the coffee and bag into the blue basket that hung from the handlebars, unlocked the bike, then stretched her arms high, a pleasant, contented look on her face.

Zach blinked once, then slumped back into his chair. No air seemed to reach him...she was just getting coffee.

As she pulled away, he followed her in a numb silence. Moments later, he watched as she turned her bike toward the President's Pavilion and stopped at the guard tower. Campus Security Officer Jones emerged, a grin taking over his jowly face. He stretched out his arms and took Lindsey into a deep hug. Then they talked for a moment, wisps of steam drifting up from their mouths. Lindsey laughed, shook her head, and then reached for the basket. She handed Jones the bag and one of the coffees, hugged him again, then rode away.

Zach pulled forward in numb silence and stopped at the gate. Inside, he saw Jones sipping from the coffee cup, a giant slab of chocolate sitting on a napkin to the side. Jones nodded absently and opened the gate as he took another sip. Zach did not drive through. He sat perplexed.

Jones tilted his head. "Good morning, Professor," he said. "Need something?"

"Um..." Zach forced a smile. "Chocolate for breakfast, huh?"

Jones smiled wide. "I know, my wife would kill

me. Don't tell."

"You're safe," Zach assured him. "Hey, was that Lindsey Monahan I just saw ride through here?"

"Yup," Jones said, taking a nibble from the chocolate. "One of yours, right? Sweet girl."

"I don't...I—"

"Right, so many new faces."

Zach nodded uncertainly. "She brings you coffee?"

"Everyday. Goes to some shop she fell in love with. Says it makes her feel like she's a real student surrounded by all the big brains." Jones laughed. "Plus, she says the coffee shop walls are covered with baskets of chocolate you buy by weight. Gets me a different chunk every morning so I can try all the flavors." Jones shook his head, as if reminding himself of a private joke, then set the chocolate down. "So, you going in, Professor?"

'Oh, yeah!" Zach laughed, then put his car in gear. "I guess I was dreaming of chocolate," he said. "Have a good day."

The words tumbled around in his mind as if they were trying to find a place to land. She was just getting coffee. He parked and walked across campus, unaware of anything other than those words. Maybe Lindsey wasn't a spy. Maybe she was just...Lindsey. Amazing Lindsey.

As Zach lumbered up the steps of the lab and down a hall, he felt himself dropping into a new reality. Maybe the simmering anxiety he felt wasn't fear of losing the Delta Program. Maybe it was fear of losing Lindsey. The thought so disoriented him that he almost didn't see Cedric and his outstretched arm, barring him from the lab door.

"Hello, daydreamer," Cedric said, leaning against the wall.

"Oh." Zach stopped. "I didn't see you there."

"I know, as much as that hurts my feelings, I am still here to warn you."

Zach blinked. "Warn me?"

"Yes. I don't have a car."

"I'm confused."

"I know. That's why I'm here. If you have heart palpitations you'll have to get someone else to drive you to the hospital 'cause…"

"You don't have a car."

"Exactly."

Zach dropped his bag and crossed his arms. "And why would I have heart palpitations?"

"All this consternation and despair, of course."

"No despair here, Cedric. Only work."

Cedric twisted his scarf around his hands and exhaled loudly. "I'm not blind, Professor. I see the way you look at Lindsey."

"Lindsey? I—"

"Don't even try it. Cedric sees all." A mischievous smile curved his lips. "She is a delicious little cupcake, isn't she?"

Zach looked up at Cedric, his jaw tense.

"What? Of course, I thinks she's attractive, who

wouldn't? Don't look at me all surprised like that. I'm not that binary."

A small laugh escaped Zach's mouth. He looked at Cedric again. "Who knew?" he said.

"Who cares," Cedric said. "Any fool can she only has eyes for you."

"I don't know what you're—"

"For a smart man, you sure are dense."

Zach felt his jaw tighten. "Don't push it."

"Like Buddha says, *'no matter how hard the past, you can always begin again.'*"

"Meaning?"

"Meaning...begin again," Cedric said, motioning toward the lab. "She's in there."

Zach shook his head as he glared through the solid lab door. "Too late."

"Okay, Professor, I say this with love and as a friend of the family. Get out of your own way. Regret sucks."

"Buddha said regret sucks?"

"No, that one's all me."

"You sound like Sam."

"Well, if that's the case then one of two things are happening: either we are both right, or it's a sign of a coming Apocalypse. Either way, what do you have to lose?" Cedric said. "Just talk to her, Professor. No IM, no text, just the two of you, eye to eye. You can manage that, right?" He walked to the door and turned the handle with a wink.

Zach felt a stirring in his belly. Maybe Cedric

was right. Maybe they could begin again. He nodded, then walked past him into the cool hum of the lab. Across the room he saw Lindsey leaned back in her chair, a giant pair of noise canceling headphones on her head. He was almost beside her when she saw him.

"Hi," she said, sliding the headphones off, her eyes like saucers, her back suddenly straight.

"Hi."

"What's up?"

Zach's mind went blank, just like the first moment he saw her. He realized then that she was the first beautiful thing he ever got stuck on. The code, and the future, and his responsibilities all evaporated. Like he'd landed in an alternate dimension. His mind raced back to how she felt in his arms, how the scent of her skin lingered for only a fleeting moment after he'd yelled and left her kneeling, half-naked, on her sofa. How he longed to slide his lips along the delicate curve of her ear and drown himself in that scent again. He forced a smile. "I've seen some good trends in your work so far."

"Um...Thanks."

"Also, I noticed your processing speeds were holding you back, so I got you a..." He looked around. "An ergonomic chair."

Lindsey's mouth pulled to the side. "Gee, but I didn't get you anything."

Zach shifted his weight onto his other foot,

trying to imagine how he would ask her to let them start again, when her phone began to rattle across her desk. Lindsey's eyes tore from his. She jumped up, grabbed the buzzing phone and bolted. "Sorry," she called over her shoulder as she headed for the door. "Gotta go."

Chapter 15: Lindsey

As soon as she heard the click of the lab door, Lindsey threw her back against the hallway wall and tried to steady her breath. The way Zach had looked at her made her heart thump wildly in her chest. As she tried to calm herself, she realized the incessant rush of pounding blood had made its way down her body to her lower torso. She squeezed her eyes shut and tried to make the feeling stop.

"Hello?" She heard a muffled voice call out. "Lindsey?"

Oh, crap, Lindsey muttered, realizing her cell phone was hanging limply in her hand. "Hi," she said, pulling the phone to her mouth. "Sorry about that."

In the glow of the screen she saw Kate's face twist. "Where are you?" She frowned. "And why are you talking like that? Are you okay? Why is your face so red?"

"Shh," Lindsey said, bringing the phone closer as if she was whispering in Kate's ear. "I don't want anyone to hear." She looked back toward the lab where she could almost feel Zach's eyes boring at her through the thick cinder block walls. She stared back, wondering if he still stood awkwardly next to her cube. He had been so close she could feel her skin tingle in response. He looked like he wanted to talk...but why now after weeks of the cold shoulder? She bit her lip, hoping he didn't know what she was up to.

"You could have just texted me—" Kate said.

"No. No, I couldn't," Lindsey said, looking imploringly into the camera. "It's—listen, Kate, I need your help."

"Now I'm really worried."

"Sorry, I didn't mean to worry you. I'm fine."

"Fine? You've been blowing up my phone. Now you're flushed and whispering in some dark hallway. Of course I'm worried."

"I'm good. I just need your spidey-sense. I need to connect some dots."

"Hold on," Kate said, anxiety draining from her face. "Is this all about your mom and her new boyfriend? What's the big deal? I think it's awesome. She deserves some fun."

"Ew. Seriously. Ew." Lindsey quivered. "Anyway, this is more important."

Kate leaned back into what looked like a giant

leather chair, concern spreading across her face. "Okay, Lindz," she said. "Hit me."

Lindsey pulled the phone to her face conspiratorially. "Good. Here's the basics. I read some weird messages to our dean, and—"

"And how did you come by these messages?"

Lindsey frowned into the screen. "Places." she gestured with her hand. "And stuff."

"Oh, God…" Kate buried her face in her hands. "You're hacking the dean? The dean of your new university?"

"Hacking? I prefer to say helping."

"I hope you're being careful."

"You know I am. Just go with me here." Lindsey took a breath as she looked down the hall to make sure no one was coming. "The dean is getting messages from this lady, but the lady doesn't exist. I found a back door to her server, and—"

"What lady? Wait. Start from the beginning."

"Yeah, sorry. So, my new friend, Cedric, found the messages first. The sender was supposedly a Boston socialite."

"Okay…"

"Well, the IP address she used to send the messages didn't match her physical location. Her social media says she's been lounging in Aruba for months. That means someone in Boston is using her log-in and her server."

"I'm not following. So what?"

"So, the messages are weird. And the dean's

response is even weirder."

"Like…how weird?"

"Okay," Lindsey said. "Don't get mad, but… Cedric installed a RAT." Lindsey saw the blank look on Kate's face and exhaled, not wanting to explain. "He installed spyware to watch the dean through her own camera. Like a hidden-camera in her own office."

Kate leans forward. "No way, you can do that?"

"Yeah, put a piece of tape over your camera. You never know."

"Jeez."

"Anyhoo, Cedric recorded the dean having meetings about university funding. She's threatening to close down the program."

"The program you're in?"

"Yes, but that doesn't matter."

"It sure as hell does!"

"Okay," Lindsey nodded. "It does. But here's where it gets weird. University financials show the university is flush this year. So why are they cutting programs?"

"Good question."

"Plus, in the messages, the two keep discussing *Elysian Fields*. The socialite keeps demanding it and the dean keeps promising it."

"What's that?"

"I don't know! But it can't be good. The emails lay out a kind of countdown clock. Whatever it is, it's overdue. Look, I have more. Can you take a peak if I email you everything? See what you can come up with?"

"Sure, Lindz, but where is this going?"

"I don't know," Lindsey whispered. "There's something hinkey going on. Someone keeps testing our security, there are glitches popping up in the code I didn't put there. It's all too weird and I'm worried about Zach..."

"Zach who?"

"Oh," Lindsey muttered, feeling her face flush. "My professor."

"You call your professor Zach?" Kate grinned. "Uh-oh." Lindsey watched as a tall blond man walked around the back of Kate's chair and kissed her lovingly on the cheek. "Lindsey has a boyfriend," Kate sang.

"Hi, Chase." Lindsey nodded into the camera.

"Hey, Lindz." He grinned. "That's great. When are you coming to visit?"

"Soon, I hope."

"Good," he said. "Kate misses you."

"I miss her."

"Boyfriend, huh?"

"It's nothing, I—" Lindsey felt hot breath on the back of her neck and spun around. "What the— James! Cut it out."

James pulled back and ran his hand through his hair before beaming over Lindsey's shoulder into the camera. "Is that your mommy?"

"What the hell?" Kate said, sitting forward.

"Your mom? Do I look like your freaking mom?"

"Who's the douche?" Chase asked.

"Hey, bro," James said, putting up his hands. "Don't be so tense."

"Do you mind?" Lindsey seethed, dropping the phone to her side. "This is a private conversation."

"Whatever," James said, opening the lab door with a flip of his hair. "Later, Lindsey."

Lindsey put her lips close to the screen as she watched James walk into the lab and close the door before turning back to face Kate and Chase on her phone.

"Sorry about that."

Kate frowned. "Is he in the program too?"

"Yeah." Lindsey smirked. "But he doesn't care. Cedric thinks he might be plotting against us, too, I just can't figure out how."

"That guy might be hurting you?" Kate turned toward Chase and they gave each other a silent nod. "Oh yea, Lindsey. We'll help."

"Thanks, Kate! I gotta go back in. I'll send you the details."

Lindsey clicked off the screen and opened the lab door. As she entered, she saw Cedric look at her expectantly from his chair. Lindsey sent him a nod and tapped the side of her nose with one finger. The game was on. She was going to find out what was going on before anyone got hurt… especially Zach.

Chapter 16: Zach

Zach opened his tired eyes and looked at the ceiling. He ran a rough hand over his face then stretched, trying to pinpoint exactly where he was. When his toes hit a filing cabinet, he knew. He had fallen asleep at the lab again.

Rumpled sheets swirled around him as he flipped onto his stomach. Cocooned in darkness, pieces of yesterday fell into place, the weight of each one becoming heavier than the last. The Delta Program was finally going well, but he couldn't hold on to any threads of happiness, he still felt crushed.

Yesterday, Lindsey turned in bridges of code— scores of code, each a scaffold building toward the master code the project needed. She worked with a zeal he had not seen before. The final pieces were coming together and he spent the night linking the chain. But as the master code emerged, his connection to Lindsey had disintegrated—and it was all his fault. He wrapped his fists into the sheets and listened to the lab. A tap-tap-tap came from the next room. He recognized the steady, gentle cadence. She was here.

Zach swung his legs over the side of the bed and gave them a hearty shake. With one hand, he grabbed the empty coffee pot and looked sideways through his office blinds. He could see the perfect curls of Lindsey's dark hair framing the long pale skin at the back of her neck. Her headphones were on, and one hand was perched above the keyboard as if she were about to crack a safe. She leaned back for a moment, took a breath and turned her head. Her brown eyes widened as she looked directly at him. She blinked, and then a small smile spread across her lips. Zach's breath caught in his chest. He forced a smile back and then dropped the blinds back into place. At least she was still smiling at him, but that was Lindsey.

Grabbing a shaving kit with his free hand, Zach opened the door to his office.

"Morning," he said.

Lindsey hit a key and her screen went black. "Good morning, Professor," she grinned, removing her headphones.

Zach felt his face drop. Her monitor had been alight until he opened the door, then she hit a boss screen. He stopped in his tracks and checked himself. She was probably just messaging friends. He pulled the empty coffee pot into view. "Want some?" he asked.

Lindsey smiled. "No, thanks. I got some this morning."

Right, Zach thought. In Harvard Yard.

Zach went out to the hall and entered the restroom. His tired eyes glared back at him from the mirror above the sink as he turned on the hot water. Steam framed his face as he ran his razor under the water. He brought the blade down along his jaw and tried to relax, wondering how much of his problems were created in his own mind. As the final stroke of the razor came down, he switched the water to cold hoping the cool water would sooth him.

He thought of his brother's words. *Sometimes it's good to get burned.* Zach gripped the sink and raised his eyes to the mirror again as the cold droplets fell. He didn't need to touch Lindsey to get burned. The very sight of her scorched him. Fire had filled his veins, but there was no way to quench it now. He had lost Lindsey forever by doubting her. She made that clear yesterday when she ran out of the room.

She wasn't a spy. She just wanted to finish college, live the dream she had lost. At least he could make sure that happened. He remembered what the dean had said: *if this project didn't come together fast, she might not get her degree at all.* He dried his face and stalked back into the lab, making a beeline for his desk. He was almost done. He would finish the code, send it to the dean, and make sure Lindsey got her degree.

Zach walked past Lindsey without a word and shut his office door. As he brought his monitors to life, memories of last night's code lapped against each other like tiny waves; he just had to find a way to connect them. He frowned as the same problems popped up. Each time he found a link, one section would unravel and the whole string would fall away. He slammed down his laptop and rubbed his eyes. It's got to be here, he muttered to himself, then heard a ding.

Zach opened his monitor again and a white square popped up in the corner. It was an IM from Lindsey.

"Are you alright?" It read.

Zach opened his blinds to see her pixie face looking at him from her desk. He turned to his keyboard.

"The data isn't syncing," he wrote, planting both feet on the floor *"We are so close!"* he continued. *"I feel like the answer is right in front of me, but I can't see it. My brain is just fried."*

He turned and looked at Lindsey through the office glass, throwing his hands up in frustration. He saw her nod, then turn toward her own keyboard. A ding soon followed.

"I think I have a solution," her next IM read.

"You do?"

"*Yes,*" she wrote, "*I'll show you. Come here.*"

Zach looked out and felt his heart begin to thump a little harder. He stood, wiped his hands against the front of his jeans, and walked out.

Lindsey spun once in her chair, then stood to face him, her mouth pulled in a serious line. "Are you willing to try something new?" she asked.

Zach felt his skin flush. "Sure," he said.

With a nod, Lindsey turned back toward her computer. She pulled up a black screen saturated with strings of green code. As the two of them stared at it, she reached out and squeezed his hand reassuringly. "Trust me?" she asked.

Zach felt the heat rising up his arm. "I do," he said.

Okay," she said, pulling him by the hand. "Step back." He followed her, and the two peered down at the screen. "Sometimes, I find if I step back, I see fresh patterns in the data," she said.

Zach squinted at the screen dubiously.

"Okay," she said, pulling him again." Now, take a step forward."

Zach followed her lead, not wanting to let go. Her hand was so soft.

"Now forward again," she said. "Now back. Now to the side," she said, pulling him by the arm. "Now cha-cha!" she laughed, grabbing him by both hands. "Now, we're dancing!"

Zach's arms curled around hers, his head falling back into a laugh.

"Twirl me! Twirl me!" Lindsey cried, and he did. He twirled her around and then pulled her close, their necks tilted down toward each other. As she laughed, he felt her breath coming rapid and hot against his neck and ear. He wasn't afraid to be burned anymore.

In a rush, he took her by the back of the head and brought his lips down on hers. Her mouth opened softly in surprise and then she pulled away. He saw a small frown of confusion pass behind her eyes, but then it faded.

"Okay," she said, gripping his hand. "Look again."

Zach blinked at her absently as he tried to remember what she meant. She pulled him by the waist and together they leaned forward. As his eyes adjusted to the screen, the code shone in a fresh, bright blue.

"See?" she asked.

"Wow." He nodded, his eyes growing wide. "I...wow. It's totally new." He should have rushed to his keyboard to get down what he saw, but he turned toward Lindsey instead. He suddenly saw new possibilities in her eyes, as well. The click of the machines serenaded them as they stood alone in the lab, looking into the other's eyes. Zach reached forward and wrapped his arms around her waist, pulling her closer. He saw her blink rapidly then tilt her lips toward his. He leaned in to kiss her again when he heard the door click open.

Cedric walked in, wide-eyed. He grinned, then took the back of his heel and slammed the lab door shut behind him.

"Cedric!" James called from the hallway. "Jeez! You shut the door right in my face!"

"Sorry, pal," Cedric called back, giving Lindsey and Zach a wink. "My bad."

Zach peeled away and got to his office door just as James walked in with a smug look smeared across his face. "Lindsey." He grinned wider as he saw her. "How's my favorite coder?"

Zach stopped short and turned to lean in his office doorway.

"Fine," Lindsey responded as she sat abruptly and wheeled her chair into her cube. "Working, you know?"

James sauntered over and leaned his hip against her desk. "Too much work, babe. Did you get my message about hitting Nicaragua for Winter Break?"

Zach coughed into his hand, trying to hide a scoff that escaped his throat. *The only reason James would go to a third world country was to play tennis and get a tan.*

James looked up at the sound. "Oh, hey, Professor."

"James."

"Anyway," James continued, leaning in toward Lindsey. "I got your message. I like a girl who makes the first move."

Zach felt his muscles tense and his back

straighten. He watched as Lindsey laughed awkwardly, then nodded.

"If your message was a booty call, I like your chances." He leered as his eyes lingered in all the wrong places. Zach felt his teeth grind as James continued. "Some friends are going to the bar tonight. Why don't you come?"

Zach saw Lindsey lean back slightly to see his face. He couldn't be sure, but he thought he saw a slight rise in her shoulders. Maybe he should go over and save her, make up some excuse about needing work done. Zach took a step forward, but halted when he heard her respond.

"Sure," she said. "What time?"

Zach fell back against the wall as the air went out of him. Lindsey was going out with James? Was that who she was messaging earlier? The taste of Lindsey's kiss still lingered on his mouth as he felt his last glimmer of hope disappear. He turned slowly and walked back into his office.

Chapter 17: Lindsey

Lindsey's sleeve stuck to the table as she tried to pull her arms back and tuck her elbows close to her sides. With a high-five and a nod, frat boys squeezed into the booth from both sides, forcing the people next to her to shimmy closer and pin her in, the smell of booze and body odor wafting across her like a veil. She absently wondered how many more people could fit in the bar before the walls burst from the inside out.

Across the beer bottles and shot glasses that littered the table, she could just make out the top of James' head making his way back toward her with a tray teetering with glasses full of some dark, dangerous looking liquor.

"Up!" he said to the row of guys next to Lindsey. "Up, let me in next to my girl."

Lindsey felt the bile rise in her throat, but

swallowed it with a smile.

"Sorry that took so long, beautiful," he said as he scooted in. "It's a zoo in here."

"I can see that," she said.

"What?" James yelled.

"I can see that," she said louder.

"Right," he laughed, drawing his arm around her shoulders. "Loud, huh?

Lindsey tried to keep her back loose. "Yeah," she said. "Crazy. Hey, speaking of crazy, what's been going on at the lab? Was it always like this?"

James focused his dull eyes on her. "You tell me," he slurred. "Like what?"

"Like, weirdness. People testing the security."

"Wheeler's just paranoid." He scoffed. "Doesn't matter. We'll be out of there soon enough."

"Yeah, but aren't you worried? Just a little?"

James slid a shot glass her way. "About what?"

Lindsey curled her fingers around the glass and looked into the oily liquid but didn't take a sip. "I don't know, like, worried somebody could get our code?"

"Hell no, babe." He sneered. "I don't believe in worry. There's no money in it."

As he stifled a drunken belch, Lindsey looked toward the bar, wishing her plan was working better. There she saw a girl flip her hair back and smile at the boy next to her. *She had to learn this damned pantomime girls had.* Turning to James again, Lindsey twisted her hair around a finger and leaned in. "Thanks for the drinks. You're so smart. I bet I could learn a lot from you."

James pulled back, his eyebrows rising. "For sure. There are so, so many things I'd like to teach you," he said, as his hand slid up her thigh.

"Like, um," she said, crossing her legs so his hand fell off, "that algorithm. That must be…some piece of work."

"You're a piece of work." He growled, pushing himself closer.

Lindsey's hands instinctively went to his chest, pushing to create some distance. "Do you have it here? Could I take a peek? I think algorithms are so…so…sexy."

"Woohoo! Listen! She thinks my algorithms are sexy," James called to his buddies, gyrating his hips into the booth for a laugh. Then he spun toward her and leaned in so close she could smell the alcohol staining his breath. "It is sexy, babe. It's big, and fast, and strong, too."

"Yeah?" Lindsey said, leaning back. "How so?"

"It pushes people right to the edge," he said, leaning in again. "It gets them just where I want them to go. I could show you…"

"The algorithm?"

"So much more," he said, his breath pouring against her cheek in bitter puffs. "I can show you the man behind the brain."

Lindsey gripped her fingertips into the vinyl seat cushion and tried not to bolt. "I'd like that," she said, trying not to inhale. "But, why don't we start with the algorithm."

James' chin receded so sharply into his neck it revealed deep lines where his spray tan had seeped. "Why do you have such a hard-on for my algorithm, Viper?"

Lindsey searched his bloodshot eyes. *Oops. I went too far*, she thought. "I just, I like math, it...it turns me on." She shrugged.

"Well, too late!" he cried, downing an already empty shot glass then turning it over to double check the contents were gone. "I sold it."

Lindsey felt the tiny hairs on her arms rise, just as she heard a familiar voice behind her.

"Ms. Monahan."

Lindsey turned. Zach was looming over their table, his jawbone like a rock. Fresh snow melted on the shoulders of his woolen pee coat and a light steam wafted up around him. His eyes landed hard on Lindsey as the table went quiet.

James broke the silence with a slurred invitation. "Professor! Look who came out of his cave. Sit down! Have a drink."

Zach shot tiny daggers at James and the sight of his arm still stretched loosely over Lindsey's shoulders. "Ms. Monahan," he said, "I need you in the lab."

"Um, right now?" she asked, lifting James' drunken arm off of her by the sleeve.

"Yes," he said, his eyes dark. "Now."

Lindsey felt the hot booth turn cold as she considered why he was there. She did a quick mental check of her system and reminded herself to stay calm. No way had he found her secret file.

"Well," she said, throwing up her hands, "guess that's it for me. Gotta go," she said, shimmying out of the booth.

"No, boo!" called out a couple of frat boys. "Dad's pissed!"

Lindsey turned as she reached the edge and looked at James. His arms were crossed and the skin around his eyes had turned a deep red. "Bye, James," she said.

James' head rolled around on his neck as his words fell loosely from his mouth. "Whatever, tease."

"Okay, that's nice," Lindsey said, grabbing her coat and turning toward Zach. "Let's go."

Zach turned on his heel and Lindsey fell in next to him, each positioning to walk first as they dodged through people to exit the bar. As they pushed out into the cold night air and passed a final rush of students, Lindsey threw on her jacket and curled her scarf around her neck. "Thanks a lot." She hissed.

Zach pushed his fists down in his pockets. "Sorry I'm messing up your new love life."

"What? What are you talking about?" She glared at him. "You can't seriously think I'm interested in James."

"You're not?"

"No!"

Lindsey watched as his eyes darted from her to the bar. He was so gruff and sexy, dammit.

"How was I supposed to know that, Lindsey? You won't even *talk* to me."

"Why do you even care?" she asked, her voice raised.

Zach exhaled. "I know what you're up to."

Lindsey's squeezed her eyes shut. *Busted,* she thought. *He did see my files. That's why he's here.* "I was going to tell you, I—"

"I *know,*" he continued, "and I get it."

"You do?"

"Yeah, you missed out on college life, and you just want to experience what you missed."

Lindsey felt her eyes crinkle. "What? No..."

"I understand." Zach shrugged. "It's just that, well, James has a creepy vibe. And I was worried."

"You were?" she asked.

"Yeah, I know it's not my place. I just—"

Lindsey threw out a hand to silence him. She felt suddenly baffled. *Was he flirting?* She had spent so much time trying to prove herself to him, she'd never considered how to react if she got another chance. Words tumbled through her mind, she had so many questions, but finally, these simple words came out. "I think it's...sweet," she said carefully.

Zach turned his face toward her. "You do?"

"Uh huh," she said, trying to organize her

thoughts. "And, you're right…about James. He is creepy. I was only here to—I just wanted to see his algorithm."

"That's it?" Zach asked, confusion twisting his brow. "Why?"

"I…I thought it might help me put something together. Like a puzzle. It doesn't matter now. He sold it."

"He did? When?"

"Don't know. I might have found out, but… *someone* showed up and pulled me out of there."

"Oops."

She nodded. "Yeah."

"I have it, you know."

"What, the algorithm?"

"I guess I could let you see it, if you want. It's his IP, but it's already in my system."

Lindsey took a breath. "No, not if it's against the rules. I would never…"

"Right." Zach nodded, his jaw tightening. "Ethics. Important."

"Super important." Lindsey nodded, rocking on her heels.

For a moment the two of them stood in silence as fat white flakes fell around them. Lindsey looked up to see Zach's eyes shining in the light of a distant car. He had a question poised on his lips as he looked down at her. "So, what's next?" she asked. "With the program, I mean."

"I don't want to talk about that now." His eyes

searched hers as if he were trying to decipher something. Lindsey felt her mouth open in response just as he reached out and took her by the hand. Gently, he raised her fingers toward his mouth and blew on them. "You're cold," he said.

"I am," Lindsey said, her heart racing. "But you have hot coffee in the lab, right?"

"I do," Zach said, with a small shake of his head. "But you don't have to...I wasn't really coming here to drag you to the lab."

"I'd like to go," she blurted. "I mean, if you're going. We could share a cab..."

Zach's lips curved into a smile. "But I drove."

"Oh," Lindsey said, anticipation swirling.

Zach smiled. "We are going to the same place..." he said. "And cabs take forever."

"Uh-huh."

Lindsey swung her shoulders and tilted her head up as she looked at him. His expression was no longer uncertain. She reached out and took him by the hand. "Let's go," she said.

Chapter 18: Zach

As Lindsey walked into the cool light of the lab, Zach felt his heart begin to pound. In the seconds it took him to turn and secure the door, he promised himself he would not squander this new opportunity. Lindsey was here; she was talking to him, and he saw possibilities in her eyes. Maybe it wasn't too late.

He turned to see her waiting in the center of the room. Her hands were clenched in front of her and one of her ankles was turned slightly, as if she might bolt. He saw a mixture of regret and hope wash across her face as he came toward her. For a moment, he just stood in front of her, their body's inches apart. Then he took her two clenched hands in his and raised them toward his chest, where he held them as he spoke. "Lindsey," he said, looking into her eyes, "earlier you asked me why I care. I can't explain it, but I have cared from the beginning.

I know I didn't handle it well." He drew her hands to his heart. "I should have trusted you."

Lindsey shrugged. "Things got weird, that's all."

"I'm sorry," he said, his eyes imploring her to forgive him. "I'm so sorry. Can I fix it?"

All hesitation left her face. "You already have," she whispered. She lowered her head and kissed the top of his fingers, one by one. As her lips touched him, Zach felt his head spin. He was twirling on the top of a pin, every inch of his skin longing to be closer to her. He raised his fingers to her jaw and lifted her lips to his, first taking in her top lip, then her bottom. The soft skin of her neck arched against his lips as they trailed down to her collar bone, then the exposed skin above her collar. With one arm, he circled her back and lifted her so her lithe body was perched above him. As her delicate skin pressed into him, he heard a soft moan escape her lips.

He pressed her against the cool concrete wall behind them and ran the fingertips of both hands roughly up the back of her thighs as he nibbled at her skin. As he did, her body clung to the now granite hard bulge that pressed against her. In unison, they began to latch onto each other, rocking their tender skin together in rhythmic, rough motions.

Zach grabbed her by the back of the knees and pulled her forward until he could feel her swell beneath him. His breath became ragged as the need to feel how wet she was competed with the need to keep grinding against her. With both hands he lifted her up and set her down, kissing her as his hands laced through the top of her pants, hungry to expose her skin to his.

As he undid her zipper, he heard her moan, and his own heart beating in his ears, but then something else. He heard keys in the door. Lindsey heard it too, because her hands tightened over his and her arms tensed. They froze in place as they listened to a voice bellow down the empty corridor outside the lab, and the lock turn.

"That chicks a butter-face. You can fuck her," the voice said as the door began to swing open. "I can do better. I always do."

Zach grabbed Lindsey's hand and pulled her into the server room, closing the door quickly behind them. She squeezed his hand back as they leaned against the door and listened, trying to slow their breathing enough to hear what was going on outside. They stood together in the dark beneath the quickly blinking lights of the machines surrounding them. Zach opened the door just a sliver and they both peeked out. They saw James and an unknown friend walk into the lab. It was at least one o'clock in the morning. James couldn't even be counted on to come to class, let alone pull late-night hours in the lab. "Is that guy everywhere?" Zach grumbled.

Lindsey giggled. "Terrible timing...terrible."

"Look, dude," his friend said, lingering by the

door as he texted, "you might not think she's hot, but I do. So whatever the hell this pit-stop is for, let's get it done so we can get back to the party."

"Keep it in your pants," answered James. "I just have to log in and grab something."

Lindsey and Zach watched as James walked over to Lindsey's terminal and booted up her system. "What the hell..." Zach whispered, reaching for the door.

Lindsey pulled him back into the darkness. "It's okay," she said clutching his hand to keep him at her side. "I've got it covered."

Zach scowled at her, his fist still curled around the doorknob.

"Trust me," she whispered. "Shh."

They looked back out and saw James plug a USB into the side of Lindsey's computer. He typed something, switched out the USB and hit the enter key. "You want to bang something good, you should see the chick that runs this system," he said.

"Hot?" his friend asked.

"Smoking. But I got a stable full of hotties."

Lindsey felt Zach tense again beside her side and she rested her hand on his bicep, giving him a little rub. "Wait," she said. "You'll see."

James pocketed his device and shut down her computer. As he did, he rubbed his crotch against her keyboard. "Poor Viper," he said, "now you'll get screwed."

"Ew," muttered Lindsey. "Now I need a new

keyboard."

James sauntered back across the lab and punched his buddy in the shoulder. "What are we waiting for? Let's go get that tail."

As the lab door closed and the lock turned, Lindsey and Zach opened the server door and crept back out into the dim lights of the lab.

Zach rushed over to Lindsey's system and turned it on. "What the hell was that?" he asked, doing a systems check. "I'm going to kill that kid."

Lindsey walked over and wrapped her arms around his shoulders. "It's okay," she said, resting her cheek against his back. "I have a fail-safe. Well, several, actually, but he isn't good enough to see them."

Zach turned and looked at her, his eyes wide.

"I like a good back-up." Lindsey shrugged. "Anyhoo, wait until he tries to download that code into his own system."

"Oh yeah?" asked Zach.

"Yup," Lindsey said. "Game over."

"Really?"

"Total annihilation."

Zach laughed and reached out, his hands resting softly on both sides of Lindsey's hips. "You are amazing," he said as he kissed her softly on the side of her neck.

"Yeah." Lindsey nodded as she leaned back. "I kind of am."

Chapter 19: Lindsey

Flakes began to fall thick and wet against Zach's windshield the moment they pulled away from the university, and as they drove, the path before them blurred. The heat of their breath fogged the windows. Lindsey sat huddled in the passenger seat, thinking. It felt so right to touch and kiss Zach in the lab, but now, in the cool night air, she considered the consequences. She glanced over at Zach and saw his beautiful jaw was clenched in thought, but then he turned to her and his face softened into a smile. He reached over and drew her hand to his mouth, kissing the back of her fingers adoringly as if he had been doing it for years. The intimacy made Lindsey's heart flail suddenly between expectation and confusion. She pulled her hand back just as he spotted a place to park.

He turned off the engine without a word and

darted around the car to open her door. His steady hand helped her onto the icy sidewalk before shutting the door behind her and curling his arm tightly through hers. As he hurried them along, fresh snow landed damp and cold against their cheeks and ears. The snow crunched beneath them with only the sliver of a new moon to light their way.

As they turned left toward their building, Lindsey stopped. She gripped Zach's hand and looked up at the darkened apartment windows and ornate iron entry. The last time they had walked through these doors together it ended in disaster.

"What are we doing?" she asked.

Zach shrugged. "I don't know. Starting over?"

Lindsey dropped her head and squeezed snowflakes from her eyes wishing his answer was more certain. Once they walked up these stairs, she knew nothing would ever be the same again, and she didn't know if her heart could take it this time. She suddenly stepped away and drew her scarf away from her neck, exposing her flushed skin to the crisp, night air.

Taking a step forward, she tilted her head back to let the fluffy flakes of snow drop down and melt against her skin. They landed against her lips and eyelids and the base of her neck and she wished suddenly the snow would double in size. She wanted it to dump all over them and not stop until they were snowed-in forever. If only they could run up these stairs and lose themselves in the warm comfort of each other's arms, she would go now and never leave. But tomorrow, the snow would melt and they'd be back in the lab, and she didn't know what would happen then.

She dropped her head and opened her eyes to see Zach staring back at her. "My God," he said, stepping forward and tracing his fingers down her cheek, "you are stunning."

The delicate touch of his fingers made her inhale sharply and close her eyes again. "Is it even possible?" she asked. "Can we... can we just start over?"

"We can," he said, taking her by the waist and kissing a fresh snowflake from her cheek. "We *should*."

Lindsey heard a note of certainty she hadn't heard before. She hoped that certainty would carry them both through, no matter what happened tomorrow. "I'd like that," she said, nodding.

"That's good," Zach said, pulling her into his arms. "Because I don't think I can stay away from you anymore."

"Then don't," Lindsey said as her resistance evaporated. "Kiss me."

Zach cupped her face gently in his hands and bent down to plant his warm, divine lips on hers. "You're cold," he murmured, kissing her again. "Let's get you inside and out of those wet clothes."

The thought made Lindsey even wetter.

Together, their feet crunched up the stairs and through the door of the building. As it swung shut behind them, the heat from the foyer mixed with the heat rising in Lindsey's chest. Once the door closed behind them, Zach turned. She felt certain he could see the steam rising from her skin.

She quickly undid the buttons of her coat and peeled it off. In seconds, she closed the gap between them and was just able to see the surprise in his eyes as her lips found his. The taste of him was so new, yet so familiar, she felt suddenly as if she had traveled a long distance just to arrive back home. "Finally," she gasped, then kissed him again. She got so lost in the feeling rising within her that she was bewildered when Zach pulled back and buried his face into her neck.

Blinking rapidly, she realized another couple had entered the building and were shaking off the snow. Lindsey followed Zach's actions and tilted her face toward his, waiting for the couple to leave. As they stood pressed together, they listened as four footsteps mounted the stairs, then entered an apartment with the turn of a key and the sound of a door shutting.

Immediately, Zach had her by the hand. Together, they practically ran up the stairs and seconds later he had opened a door and they were inside, alone in the dark entrance of his apartment. Before Lindsey could speak, he pulled off both of their sweaters and tossed them to the side before planting his lips back onto hers. She closed her eyes and wrapped her arms around his back, relishing the slight prickle of the evening stubble that had grown around his mouth and chin. Her fingers gripped the velvety hair on the back of his head as she kissed him, her mouth hungry to taste him, to feel him against her, and inside of her.

As Zach tilted her head to plant tender wet kisses down her neck and chest, she felt her blood rise.

"You won't leave this time?" She panted.

"I wouldn't do that," he said, switching to the other side of her neck.

"You did last time we were here."

His head fell forward as his hands gripped her hips in despair. He took a labored breath as his eyes drew up and looked into hers. "This time is different," he said. "You're stuck with me. Plus, this is my apartment. You would have to leave me."

Lindsey smiled. "That's not going to happen."

"Promise?" he whispered as he pushed himself all the way against her and let her feel the full length of his desire. He began to nibble butterfly kisses down her ear lobe and across her neck. "Promise?" he asked again, his breath hot in her ear.

"Yes, I—" Lindsey tried to say as he switched to the other side of her neck. "Yes—" His lips covered her mouth as she clung to him, urging him closer. Her mouth broke free. "Take me to bed," she said.

In one swift move, he lifted her into his arms

and carried her into a darkened bedroom, setting her down on the soft fabric of the sheets. Then he crawled across the bed and laid the length of his body against her. In the dark, she could just make out his eyes, shining and aflame at the vision of their half-nude bodies together again. The look of desire in his eyes made Lindsey pulse with a new, wet urgency. Her fingers rushed to pull off his pants, revealing the exquisite skin across his powerful thighs and groin.

He peeled off the last of her clothes, and within seconds, their skin was fully bare and touching. A desperation revealed itself that had been building for weeks. There was no preamble. She spread her legs to welcome him, the intense need to be one with him engulfing her. She clutched at the taut skin of his lower back and urged him closer. In turn, he laced his fingers through hers and pulled her arms high over her head.

"Lindsey," he whispered simply, then slid into her, agonizingly slow so she could feel every inch of him. Electricity thrummed through her, making her clench and spin and her muscles tighten.

She cradled him with her legs and arms, taking him deeper as he began to glide in and out, their bodies creating a swelling, hot friction that she felt might make them both explode into a million pieces. Joy grew within her as the slow, aching rhythm increased, and her fingers ripped from his and gripped his lower back and buttock, urging him deeper. She circled her hips up into him, making them both wet and slick with sweat as they charged together into the warm waves of pleasure.

Then, he slowed. With a whimper, Lindsey opened her eyes. Zach was staring down at her, his soul bared. She was right, nothing would ever be the same again. She craned her neck and kissed him, her chest swelling as another sweet layer was added to a moment that felt already perfect.

Zach kissed her across her face and neck then sunk his arms beneath her back, holding her totally as he began to grind into her again, the vibrating sensation of heat and friction growing between them as their bodies rocked. He was so deep, and she felt so safe and loved, that a profound throbbing began to overwhelm her whole body. With every motion, Zach was telling her something she had always wanted to hear, and her body blossomed in response. A cry she had never heard escaped her lips as she arched up and almost bucked him off the bed and exploded beneath him. As she did, his body went rigid and then suddenly still against her until they remained motionless against each other, their breath jagged and rushing with the beat of their two hearts.

Chapter 20: Zach

"No," Zach said. "Seriously?"

"Yes," Lindsey said, stroking the back of his bare leg with the delicate tips of her fingers. "That happened. So funny."

"A pole? An actual stripper pole?"

"Yup, that's my mom," Lindsey said, pulling the sheets over them and beginning to trace the tips of each of his fingers with her own. "Actually, I'm happy for her."

Zach curled his arms around the soft, naked skin of her torso and pulled her closer, sinking into the sweetest feeling he had ever known. Their torsos and limbs cupped together perfectly. He quieted his breath to listen to her heart beating steadily beside him, keeping time with the words of thankfulness streaming through his head.

"It's just her time," Lindsey said as her hands

flattened softly against his back. "I just don't know what comes next for me, you know? I thought I would just go back home after I finished here. Now, there is no home."

"You have a home now," Zach said, kissing her temple.

"Sure, today. But I have to figure out what to do after graduation, when the project is over."

"Baby," he said, enjoying the word on his lips, "opportunities are endless for you."

"I don't know," she said softly. "Maybe..."

"Maybe? Are you kidding? You're amazing. The things you can do with code, it's...it's remarkable."

"I'm great in my lane, sure. But let's remember, the first time I tried to get my degree, I cracked."

"You were a kid," he said, kissing the top of her head. "And you're doing it now."

"I am." She smiled against his neck. "I finally got unstuck, you know?"

Zach nodded. He knew how she felt. He was stuck, and didn't even know it until Lindsey arrived and changed everything. In a rush, he bent down and kissed her, feeling her lips open and slide against his own. She was a lush, moist oasis in the arid desert that had become his life. He hadn't realized how thirsty he was until he tasted her. "You are so much more than you give yourself credit for, Lindsey," he said gently. "The world needs you."

"The world, huh?" She giggled, tossing the

sheets off of them and revealing the bright morning light.

"Yes, the world," he said, sitting up on one elbow. "You are special, don't you realize that?"

Her face fell and she shook her head against the back of her pillow. "You're the special one. You care so much about helping people."

Zach shot up in bed. "What time is it?"

Lindsey turned and grabbed her phone. "7:47. Why?"

Zach swung his legs over the bed. "I have a meeting. Gotta go."

Lindsey reached out and grabbed his arm. "Wait, Zach," she said. "Not yet."

He looked back at her, her dark hair ruffled against the white of the sheets.

She stretched out her arms. "I want to hold you for five more minutes."

Zach looked at the door, then at Lindsey's skin, and couldn't leave. He swung his legs back under the sheets and stretched into her arms. He curled himself so tightly around her that, for a moment, he couldn't tell whose limbs were where. In the silence he pressed his head against hers and drank in the warmth of her skin.

"You know," she whispered, "all this pressure you feel, this burden you carry, you don't have to do it alone."

His heart swelled. "I have to say something, Lindsey."

"Okay," she said, stroking his arms.

"That first week, when you said someone bleached the files. I thought that was—I thought you were hacking me."

Lindsey's body stiffened beside him, but she did not speak. Zach pressed himself against her and cradled the back of her neck with his hand. "I'm sorry, I was wrong. I can trust you. I know that now."

She sat up and held the sheet to her breast. "Don't apologize. I've done things—"

"I know, but everything you do is to help people, too."

She shook her head, her fists balled up in the sheets. "No...well, yes. Listen—"

Her phone dinged. She reached for it then turned the screen away from him. "Oh no," she said.

"Is that your mom?" Zach asked, jumping out of bed. "More drama about the new boyfriend?"

Lindsey frowned before nodding. "Uh huh."

Zach bent down to kiss her. "See you later?" he asked.

She nodded again.

"Okay, baby. I gotta get in the shower, I have to see the dean."

Zach turned back to see Lindsey's anxious face before he entered the bathroom. "Don't worry," he called as he turned the taps, "it's just a check-in. I should be back this afternoon." As he stepped into the rush of hot water, her name played on his lips. Lindsey, Lindsey, Lindsey. He dried quickly and popped back into the bedroom to kiss her goodbye, but he found only an empty swirl of crumpled sheets. He listened to the apartment above, but didn't hear anything. She must have gone to the lab.

Zach dressed and jogged down the stairs to his waiting car. Moments later, he was rushing into the dean's office, ten minutes late.

"I hope that ridiculous grin means you have good news for us, Professor," he heard the dean say as he opened her door.

Zach stopped abruptly as President Sanders swiveled in a chair to give him a nod.

"Hello," Zach stopped. "I didn't know the president would be joining us."

"I'm afraid he must," Dean Cruz said, her hands pressed into her desk, "to witness the conversation."

Zach's head turned from the dean to the president as he let the door close with a thud behind him. "Alright," he said carefully.

"Please, Professor, sit down," the president said amiably, pointing at the empty chair by his side. "Not to worry."

Zach nodded, but knew better.

The dean flipped open a paper file and scanned it before clutching together her glossy fingernails and scowling. "We need to discuss some... unorthodox behavior coming from your team."

"Unorthodox? How?"

"I've interviewed some of your students. I understand there are parties in the lab. Alcohol. Fraternization that is, no doubt, delaying results."

Zach fell back into the chair. "You can't be serious. You have pretty much just laid out the definition of *college*."

She smirked. "Perhaps, but other college programs don't have as much on the line as yours. This is not a vanity project. I have made it clear, in order to keep your funding going, we must see results, and you have allowed behavior that has hindered those results."

Zach began to grind his jaw. "We have gotten results. We just need—"

"What? What do you need from me, more time? Again?" Zach watched as a bright pink rash bloomed across the dean's chest and throat. Her hand flew up to her jewel encrusted necklace, which she rubbed as if for solace. "Or do you need new servers? Because we gave you that. Or do you need another stray cat to come in at the eleventh hour?"

The muscles in Zach's legs tensed as if they would force him up and out of his chair. "Are you referring to Lindsey Monahan? Are you calling her a stray cat?"

"The other students don't like her, and she hasn't produced anything of value. If I had my way, I would remove her immediately."

Zach's eyes flitted to the president, whose eyes

were watery and downcast. Apparently, he wasn't here to help. Zach turned back and stared straight at the dean. "How would you know?"

"Know what?"

"That Lindsey hasn't produced anything."

The dean dabbed her tongue into the corners of her mouth. "Because you haven't shown us anything. Are you saying she has?"

"Yes!" he said, then revised his tone. "Yes. Amazing results. Results that will lead us to success. I have no doubt."

A smile stretched across the dean's face, which pulled her temples strangely into the corners of her hair. She leaned back and clucked. "Well, alright then. We will extend your program for one more month, until the end of this semester."

"A month?" Zach blurted. "That's not enough —"

"No more excuses," the dean said. "We weren't planning to give you even that. Moreover, I expect a weekly update with a copy of your work in progress."

"What good would that do? Do you even read code?"

"If we don't see results, your program will end. Am I clear?"

Zach's head whipped toward President Sanders. "Do you agree with this?"

The old man coughed and leaned on the arm of his chair. "I suppose." he said. "Time has flown by,

Professor. I suppose we just…we need to be more in the loop. That would assuage concerns. A month seems fair."

"One month?" Zach repeated, trying to organize all his thoughts.

"Yes," said the dean. "Now we understand each other."

Zach closed his eyes for a moment, remembering Lindsey standing in the evening snow, her head tilted back as flakes fell softly on her face, a quiet hopeful smile on her lips. He was so struck by her beauty and vulnerability he could barely catch his breath. He imagined how she would look if she was told the project had failed and her dream was crushed. He wouldn't let that happen.

Zach took a breath and slowed his heart rate before standing. "If you'll excuse me, I've got work to do."

Without looking back, Zach rushed out the door and across the quad.

Chapter 21: Lindsey

"I can't do it," Lindsey said, clutching Cedric's arm. "I can't." As she stared down the hallway, black spots began to rise up against the pale linoleum.

"You're hurting me," Cedric said evenly, pulling away.

"Oh!" Lindsey sputtered. "Sorry. I'm just—"

"Center yourself." Cedric said, his calm eyes gazing down at her. "He has to know."

Lindsey's lungs contracted so tightly she couldn't get a breath. "I can't. I don't want to hurt him."

Cedric put two calming hands around her shoulders. "It will all work out. Believe that. Strive on with diligence, girl."

Lindsey shook out her fingers and took the deepest breath she could. "Okay," she said. "Let's do it quick before I lose my nerve."

A muffled beat grew as they walked toward the lab. As she pushed the door open, music washed over them like a rush of air. The lab was dark except the lights cast from Zach's office, the walls of which were lightly shaking with the thump of old school hip-hop.

Lindsey stepped forward. "Zach?"

Zach's head popped up from behind his bank of monitors. His hair was standing up in all directions, and his face was covered with more than a two-day stubble. At the sight of her, his hands shot up in the air. "Lindsey! Fantastic timing!" he said, rushing out his office door. Lindsey's hands dropped to her sides as Zach jogged up to her. His hands grabbed both sides of her face, he smiled, and then his lips pressed onto hers. "You're here." He grinned.

"I'm here too," said Cedric. "Where's my kiss?"

Zach turned. "Sorry, buddy," he said, giving Cedric a bear hug then grabbing him by the shoulders. "I did it," he said, then turned again to Lindsey. "I did it."

Lindsey frowned when she saw his eyes were hooded and red. "Did what, baby?"

"I cracked it," he said grabbing her again, his arms wrapping around her. "I cracked the code."

"Oh," Lindsey said, "that's—"

Zach kissed her again, happiness radiating through his skin. "No," she said, pulling back. "Don't kiss me."

"What?" Zach asked, bewildered. "What do you mean, don't kiss you?"

Lindsey took a breath before continuing, a frown creasing her forehead. "You can't," she said. "You won't want to."

"What," Zach asked, stepping forward. "What are you talking about, of course —"

"No." Lindsey stomped her foot. "I have to tell you something." She watched his eyes widen as he stepped back. "If you don't ever want to see me again, I'll understand..."

Zach looked from Lindsey to Cedric. "What? What's going on?"

Lindsey blinked, trying to stop tears from pooling. She opened her mouth, but no words came out. Her eyes darted toward Cedric then back to Zach.

Cedric stepped forward. "What she's trying to say is...you in danger, Professor."

Zach dragged his hand through his hair, then crossed his arms and widened his stance. "What?"

Lindsey met his eyes. "I...the bleaching wasn't me, it wasn't. Someone else bleached those files. But even after you told me not to dig...I did. I couldn't help myself."

"Go on," Zach said as a vein appeared on his temple.

Lindsey's words tumbled out. "I put a bad USB in all the lab computers to override the firewalls and get reports on everything. Everything going in and everything going out."

Zach's mouth dropped open. "Mine too?"

She sniffed. "Sorry."

Zach shook his head as if a sudden pain had run through his torso. "You did not."

"Sorry," she said again, unable to keep the tears from falling.

Cedric stepped forward. "Keep going, girl."

Lindsey nodded. "Well, it turns out, the files weren't being bleached, they were being siphoned. Someone was just picking at the edges so we wouldn't notice, taking pieces of our code piece by piece. Problem is, there was an error in their program that corrupted the file on the way out. And they left a signature."

"Yeah," Cedric said. "Like a stupid criminal who drops his driver's license at the crime scene. And I'll give you one guess who." Before there was time for Zach to answer, Cedric went on. "James, you right."

Zach dropped his head into his hands and groaned. "So, James has stolen pieces of our code?"

"Looks that way," Lindsey said.

Zach shook his head once before his jaw tensed. His shoulders and arms strained the fabric of his shirt as he began to pace slowly from one side of the lab to the other. He stopped, gripped his hands into fists and began to pace faster. Suddenly, his hands dropped and his body turned toward Lindsey. He rushed toward her.

"Thank God for you, Lindsey," he said, embracing her. "Thank God." He kissed her roughly, then took her face in his hands. "I was just about to upload the new code to my computer." He shook his head. "If you hadn't come in, he would have it all."

Lindsey blinked. "So you don't hate me?"

"No," Zach said, pulling her close. "I love you."

"You do?" Lindsey asked, her tears drying on her cheeks. "Yay! I love you!"

"I guess I'll just sit over here, all quiet and alone and stuff," Cedric mumbled.

Zach pulled Lindsey in, his breath humming against her neck. "You have perfect timing," he said. "I won't upload the master program. I'll just send it directly to the dean, then you can stay and we will just move forward." He beamed. "Together."

Lindsey leaned back. "What do you mean *I can stay*?"

Zach laughed. "Well, Dean Cruz threatened to pull our funding and your spot if we didn't get the code to her this month. Why do you think I've been in here, working for days?" he asked, grazing a finger across her cheek. "You have to graduate."

Cedric leaned against a terminal. "Like the dean can even read code," he said.

"Yeah," Zach nodded. "That's what I said. I guess James could try, but what he has he couldn't sell, it's incomplete."

"James won't have to sell it," Lindsey said. "Brenda True will."

Zach pulled away and looked down at her. "What? Who the hell is Brenda True?"

Lindsey threw a glance at Cedric. "Your turn," she said.

Cedric moved forward, then rested all his weight against one hip. "So, here's the thing, Professor, there's more…I hope you'll still love me, too."

"Oh, God," Zach said.

"Yeah, so, I put a spy cam on the dean."

"Shit."

Cedric shrugged. "She's just such a freaky bitch, you know. I wanted to see inside the crypt, watch her bake children into pies or whatever she does at night. Anyway," he continued, "she *is* into some freaky shit, a discussion for another time, I think, but she is definitely in cahoots with James and some chick named Brenda True. My guess is Dean Freaky is selling the algorithm to Brenda T and taking a cut."

Zach's arms fell loosely to his side. He blinked rapidly, then rushed to his office. Lindsey and Cedric ran behind him, watching his fingers fly across his keyboard. Within seconds, search engines and websites illuminated his screens.

"What?" Lindsey asked rushing in behind him. "What is it?"

"I know that name," Zach said, his hand

swiping his mouse across the desk. In a moment, Brenda True came up. "See?" he asked, pointing. "She's on the new donor list."

"That must be how Dean Cruz knows her," Lindsey said.

"Follow the money," Zach blurted, his fingers racing.

"What?"

"It's what my brother always says. Follow the money." He swiveled around. "Where did Brenda True get her money?"

Lindsey blinked. "A trust. My friend, Kate—you remember Kate, the PR guru? Kate found ties to a trust. I guess that's how she's able to spend all her time on a beach in Aruba."

"And your friend Kate didn't wonder why a woman of leisure, who spends her time on a beach, would want to get her hands on James' algorithm?"

"I didn't think to ask her that." Lindsey said, pulling her lips tight. "Scoot over."

Lindsey took control of Zach's keyboard and began typing. Across the screen flew public filings for the States and the Caribbean. Documents filled the screen, each overlapping the last, until Lindsey stopped the flow with a click of her mouse. She stood and looked at the screen. "Here. Here it is," she said. "The trust is paid through a company called Blackburton. Zach? What's the matter?" she asked. "What's wrong?"

Zach fell against the wall, blood draining from

his face. "No," was all he said.

Cedric wrung his hands. "Now you're even freaking me out, Professor. Spill."

"Blackburton is a defense contractor," he said quietly. "Known for their work in Global Instability Modeling."

"What would they want with a shopping algorithm?" Lindsey asked.

"That's not it," said Cedric quietly, "is it? They weren't trying to buy James' algorithm…they were trying to buy our code."

"No," Zach said, his eyes glistening. "I think they want it all."

"All of what?" Lindsey asked, her voice rising. "I don't get it."

Zach turned his beautiful eyes on her. "Our code, plus James' algorithm, could be very, very dangerous."

Lindsey swallowed. "How?"

"Our code makes it easier to learn all about people and their needs and thoughts in real time. If you add in some psycho-graphics, and an algorithm that quantifies exactly how far people can be pushed…"

"Oh, my God," whispered Cedric.

"Right," Zach said. "They can tailor make internet Bots designed to sway public opinion, disrupt dissent, and turn people against each other. They can weaponize the data and use it to control the masses. Devour power."

"Holy crap," Lindsey said. "That must be Elysian Fields."

"What?" asked Zach.

"Elysian Fields. That's what Brenda T is trying to get from the dean. And there's a countdown clock."

"Oh, my God," Zach said.

Lindsey laughed nervously. "Well, crisis averted, right?" she said, turning from Zach to Cedric. "They didn't get it."

Zach grimaced. "The dean won't stop. If we don't deliver, she'll get rid of us and put in a team that will."

Lindsey stood beside him, bewildered. "But, we can't give it to her. We *won't*, right?"

"No," Zach said, squeezing her hand. "But we have work to do. We have to create a ghost code."

Chapter 22: Zach

Zach felt Lindsey slip out of bed and tip-toe to the bathroom. In the dim light of the morning, he saw the shadow of her tiny footsteps on the linoleum within. With the whine of a pipe, his shower rumbled to life and began to let steam out through the crack in the open door.

He gripped the edge of the bed and stretched his long limbs to the very corners of the mattress. His head and eyes ached from all their work the night before, but his heart felt warm. In the last dark hours of the morning, he and Lindsey had walked hand in hand up the staircase to his apartment, falling into bed without a word. The code was done, only time would tell if their plan would work.

As he listened to the droplets of water fall, he thought of Lindsey in the lab. He had never seen anyone so fluid, so in control of the code. He and

Cedric stood and watched as she conducted the system like a maestro, the zeros and ones flying across the screen, creating her own personal symphony. Watching her made his heart swell, and then wrench tight with fear. After she graduated, the opportunities would come pouring in. As much as he wanted to hold on to her and keep her safe in his arms, he knew that would be selfish. She was an anomaly, the kind of mind that came along once in a generation, and she must be free to see where her talent would take her. His program was just the beginning.

Zach slid his feet to the floor and stood. As he did, all the blood in his body seemed to rush to his penis. He made his way across the floor and opened the bathroom door, feeling the warm, humid air rush around him. Lindsey's limbs and torso glowed from inside the glass shower stall, her body turning as she heard him enter. He gripped the side of the shower door and slid it open, his eyes cascading over her shining, long limbs.

Lindsey ran her hands over her wet hair and reached out to him with a smile. He took her hand, stepped into the hot, racing flow of the water and wrapped his arms fully around her. As he did, she stretched up toward him, wrapping her delicate fingers around the back of his neck, pulling his mouth down to hers.

Her lips were like rose petals beneath him, soft and red, stroking his mouth with her own. He heard himself let out a tiny sigh against her mouth, as she hooked one leg around him, sliding the very tip of him inside of her.

He felt a sudden need, the raw, pounding need he felt every time he entered her, creating a desperate thirst only her body could quench. He grabbed her beneath each buttock, raising her hips up to his, then buried himself within her. Her ankles curled around his back, the muscles in her thighs clutching at him, swirling, thrusting onto him. He pushed her against the wall and felt the slick velvet shroud of her flesh envelope him fully.

The pleasure of her skin against his was intoxicating, and again, he heard her name tumble out of his lips. "Lindsey," he moaned, "Lindsey." As he spoke, he felt her body begin to quiver beneath him, her nails digging into the skin on his back and neck. In a rush, he felt her body clench and shudder, her head thrown back with a look of terrible pain and pleasure. His hands gripped at her slender hips as he took her in, overwhelmed by the beautiful vulnerability of her face and body. He felt himself begin to lose control, but did not let up his feverish pace. With every stroke, he wanted his body to sing to her and tell her he loved her.

Lindsey trembled as she raised her head. Her eyes opened, and her beautiful face looked into his eyes and saw him completely. As rivulets of water dropped from her eyelids to her lips she spoke. "I love you," she said.

Zach buried his head in her neck hoping the water would mask the water in his eyes. Without planning to, he began to speak. "I'll think of this," he said into her neck, "tomorrow and the next day. I'll think of this moment, and your body, and the taste of your skin, and how it feels to be buried inside of you." Then a primal impulse surged through him and he ground their bodies together, his manhood slamming into her rhythmically, again and again until their limbs began to shake and Lindsey moaned in a way he had never heard before.

As the exhilaration of their union throbbed full and fast, Zach screamed in agony, knowing as soon as this moment was over, he would long for her again.

Chapter 23: Lindsey

Lindsey walked the final steps to the lab, a constant tingling sensation mixing with the ache between her legs. She wondered absently if other women felt this way after a morning of love making, but decided no. How would anything ever get done, then? She could barely function or think and didn't even care. Her body had sunk into a happy, vibrating bliss. She pushed open the door to find Cedric leaning against his terminal in a cowboy hat and chaps.

"Hey, girl," Cedric called out from his desk.

Lindsey dropped her bag and grinned. "Hey, Cedric. Nice hat."

"Thank you, little lady," he said, swiping a hand across the rim. "I figure this is one crazy rodeo and we are about to see the clown, so why not?"

"Where do you get all these clothes?"

"This lil' get up? I made it, of course."

"No."

"Oh, yes, sewing stops me from channeling my nervous nighttime energy toward more nefarious pastimes. I could make you something," he offered.

"I'll think about that," she said, dragging her bag by the handle to her cube and sitting down.

"I see you spent the night with the professor again." Cedric sang out.

Lindsey shot him a look. "How would you know, nosy?"

Cedric looked at her flatly. "You have a big old fuck-knot in the back of your hair."

Lindsey's hand shot up and touched a tangled section of hair above her neck. "Oh, jeez," she said, combing her short hair out with the tips of her fingers.

"I told you." He grinned, curling his thumbs into his belt loops. "Cedric sees all."

"I'll remember that." Lindsey smiled. "Any sign of you know who?"

"Not yet."

Lindsey sighed and drummed her hands on the desk. "What are you working on over there?"

Cedric turned his monitor her direction. "Entering to win a sweepstakes vacation."

"Oh, yeah? Where to?"

"Everywhere. It's a world cruise. I figure, why not enter? I'm an optimist." He grinned coyly. "Also, I built a program that has entered me 2.3 million times. By my calculations, I should win 16.4

times."

Lindsey stared wide-eyed. "Um, wow. That's..." She smiled. "Good for you."

"Yeah, it's my graduation present to myself. I am going to look so good lounging on the deck, holding colorful drinks with tiny little umbrellas. Want to enter? We could go together."

"Nah. I want to finish what I started, first. I'll celebrate after," she said.

"Well, like Buddha said, 'The only constant is change, girl'."

"I guess that's true," Lindsey murmured.

The door pushed open and in walked Zach, followed closely by James. Zach gave Lindsey a wink, then walked straight to his office, as usual.

James staggered toward his desk, reeking of last night's alcohol, bumping into Cedric's chair as he passed.

"Hey, James," Cedric called, "rough night?"

"You know it." He snickered. "But she'll survive." Then he sniffed loudly, coughed, and turned on his system.

From behind James, Cedric tapped a long finger against his nose. Lindsey nodded then pulled up a clone of James' screen. As James' fingers worked on his keyboard, Lindsey watched the code he typed, then brought up a second window and sent an instant message to Zach and Cedric.

"He's in," she typed.

"Is he buying it?" Zach typed.

"I can see him," Cedric wrote. "His face is as vacuous and obtuse as ever."

"Wait..." Lindsey typed. "He stopped. He's going online. I don't know how he could have seen our trojan this fast, he – " A moment went by, then she added. "Never mind. He's just downloading porn."

"FROM MY SERVERS?!?!?" Zach typed.

"Let him. It's all being saved in the same file," Lindsey wrote.

"Dumb ass," wrote Cedric.

"He's done!" Lindsey wrote. "He took it!"

Lindsey hit a key and her boss screen flew up as James closed his terminal and stood, stretching his hands over his head with a yawn. He pulled up his pants then grabbed his bag before heading toward the door. "Later," he called out, then walked into the hall.

Lindsey, Cedric, and Zach sat silently for several moments, then converged in the center of the lab.

"He bought it?" Zach asked.

"I think so," said Lindsey. "Now we only need the dean to buy it. I bet you a dollar James is walking straight to her office."

"I'll send her the fake demo code now."

"My malware is still installed on her system. I'll remote in to see her reaction." Cedric informed them.

Zach frowned, but then his face went slack. "Good idea." He shrugged. "Can I watch?"

Chapter 24: Zach

Zach dropped the blinds as Lindsey and Cedric wheeled in two more chairs. "Check again," he said.

Lindsey pulled out her phone. "James is still at the bar. Pics of shots were just posted."

"Okay," Zach said, stretching out his fingers then shaking his arms. "Cedric, you good?"

"Always," Cedric responded, propping up his laptop and hitting a key. The dean's office sparked into view. "But hold on, one more thing..." he said, pulling out his briefcase and propping it open against the wall. "A Mojito Sparkler seems fitting," he said, cutting limes and squeezing them into three glasses, followed by bits of fresh mint. "We will either be celebrating or drowning our sorrows before this night is over. Either way," he said, muddling the mint and pouring in the rum, "I knew cocktails would come into play."

"I won't say no," said Zach, taking a sip. "Ooh, that's good. Alright, let's do this."

Zach pulled up a copy of the ghost code, his eyes scanning the work one last time. On another screen he pulled up Dean Cruz's email address. He wrote, *"Here is your demo-program."* Then attached the ghost code to the email. His finger hovered unmoving over the send button as he took a breath and reached for Lindsey with his other hand. She gripped his fingers and gave him a little nod. He looked at Cedric, the three in silent agreement as Zach hit send.

Zach dropped back in his chair and stared at the screen. "Now we wait?"

"Now we wait," agreed Cedric, clinking the rim of his glass against the others.

Zach stroked the back of Lindsey's fingers with his thumb. She looked at him, her wide eyes glistening as she gave him a small smile.

"Here she comes," whispered Cedric, leaning forward.

The three stared at Cedric's laptop and watched through her camera as the dean rounded the side of her desk and sat on the edge of her chair. Her eyes beat down on the screen. Her red nails flew to the keyboard, opening the ghost file then scrutinizing its contents, her eyes scrolling left then right, her eyebrows straining to move as her eyes widened.

"Is she buying it?" asked Lindsey, her legs bouncing against her chair.

"Maybe," Zach said. "I hope so."

The three watched in silence as the dean leaned back, stroking the chain around her neck as she considered the file's contents. She leaned forward, grabbed her cell phone, typed something, and then tossed it back on her desk.

"What is she doing?" asked Zach.

"She must have texted James," Lindsey said, checking her tablet. "He just posted he's leaving the bar. That can't be coincidence."

Cedric smirked. "She can't read the file. She needs James to verify. Well," he said, leaning toward the bottle, "refill, anyone?"

The three sipped their remaining cocktails in silence, watching the now empty chair of the dean through her computer camera. The crackling of an overhead light broke the silence, and every few minutes, Cedric would sigh and shift in his chair. A moment later, voices could be heard.

"This better be good," said a man's voice.

"Relax," said the dean, coming into view. "You make sure this is good for me, and I'll make sure your night is good for you."

She stood behind her chair as James came into view, hoodie pulled up over his head. He sat down and peered at the screen. As he did, the dean lowered his hoodie and began stroking the back of his hair with the talons on her fingers. "You're drunk again, you bad, bad boy."

"Ew," Lindsey said.

"Oh, my God," Zach said.

"Told you," Cedric said. "Freaky bitch."

James rolled his eyes as the dean leaned over his shoulder and began running her nails over his chest. "Well?" she asked in his ear.

"One second," James said, twisting his neck away from her lips. "Let me work."

Her hands pulled back and rested above his shoulders on the top of the leather chair, her fingers tapping, and her red mouth curved into a hook.

"It looks legit," James said. "But, I'd have to test it."

"Shit!" Zach said.

"No, no, no," Lindsey cried. "Is he that good? Can he tell it's a fake?"

"Hold on," Cedric said. "The freak is on the prowl."

The three watched as the dean dragged her red nail across the top of the chair and walked around so she was facing James. "No time for that now," they heard her say. With her back to the screen, the dean lifted up the back of her pencil skirt and straddled James, pinning him back against the leather of the chair.

Zach's hand darted out and shut the laptop. "I —" He swallowed. "Sorry, I didn't want to see that."

"Yeah," Lindsey and Cedric mumbled simultaneously. "Gross."

Cedric reached for his case without a word and

refilled their glasses. They sipped in silence as the moments went by.

"Do you think it's safe to take a peek?" Cedric asked.

"No!" Zach and Lindsey said together, holding the top of the laptop closed.

"Fine," Cedric said falling back in his chair. "Then we wait."

Lindsey reached for Zach and caressed his forehead. "Don't worry," she said softly. "Everything will work out fine."

"Do I look worried?"

"A little."

"Well," Zach said turning toward her. "I know how to fix that. I can just look at you." He took her hand and planted a soft kiss on her palm.

"I guess that's my queue," Cedric said, standing to pack up his cocktail kit. "Let me know if you find out anything else. As for me, I'm going to take a hot, hot shower and try to scour the vision of the dean and James out of my head." He turned to go when a ping was heard.

All three swung toward Zach's computer. "It's her," he said, pulling his mouse over the message. "This is it..."

Chapter 25: Lindsey

Lindsey, Zach, and Cedric huddled close together to read the dean's email. *"Good work,"* it read. *"Your team may continue."*

The three stood without speaking, each blinking and re-reading the message in the dim light of Zach's office. Lindsey looked from the screen to Zach and back again, her heart racing.

"So," Cedric said, "she bought it? She bought it, right?"

Zach exhaled and put his hands on his hips. He squinted at the email as if he wanted to yank it off the screen and turn it over in his hands to examine it. "I think—I mean...I guess so."

Lindsey swallowed. "So, crisis averted? The good guys win? And I get to graduate after all?"

Zach turned to her as a wide smile spread across his face. "Of course, you'll graduate." He beamed.

Lindsey jumped up and threw her arms around his neck, kissing him suddenly on the mouth. "Yeah!" she said, clutching his shoulders. "We did it! We did it!"

"Wait," Cedric said. "There's an attachment."

Zach leaned forward and grabbed his mouse. "It's a party invitation." Zach laughed. "God, she really did buy it. Hey, Cedric, want to go drink with the dean?"

"Hell no," Cedric said, his face twisted. "You go drink with her."

"How about you, baby?" Zach said to Lindsey. "Want to drink with—Lindsey? What is it?"

Lindsey crossed her arms and began to bite her lip. "That seemed easy…"

Zach and Cedric stopped smiling. They scanned each other's faces to find reassurance. For a moment, they said nothing, then Cedric laughed. "Of course it was easy," he said. "She's not us. She wouldn't spot a hack if it popped up and smacked her like a fish."

"True," Zach said, his eyes darkening, "but it was pretty easy."

"Right?" Lindsey asked. "I mean, how can we be sure? It is kind of a big deal, right?" she said. "Maybe I'm just being paranoid."

"No," Zach said, his jaw tightening. "You're right. We can't just drop it. We have to find out."

"And how would we do that, Professor?" Cedric said, his arched eyebrows spiking. "Go ask her?

Like, '*Um, hello Freaky D, did you believe that bullshit we sent you was real? Just checking.*'"

"No," Zach turned. "We hack back in."

Cedric's mouth dropped open. "You…" he asked, "want to hack the dean?"

Zach shook his head. "It's the only way. Then we can see if she's unpacked it and sent it to Brenda True."

"Seriously?" Lindsey asked, her voice rising. "What if she sees us?"

Cedric dropped his martini case and popped his knuckles. "I'll reconfigure the root directory so only we can use it," he said. "Even if she saw it, she wouldn't know it was us."

Lindsey reached out for Zach. His hand had balled into a fist at his side. With her fingers she unclenched his fist and held his hand firmly in hers. "That should work," she said.

"Alright," Zach said, "but do it carefully."

Cedric sat, then swung his head from side to side until they heard his spine crack. Then he stretched his long fingers over Zach's keyboard and began to type. As multiple windows flashed and dropped against the monitor, Zach and Lindsey stood behind him, their arms wrapped tightly around each other's waists.

The screen flashed green and then black as Cedric built a new back door into the dean's system.

"Wait," Zach said as Lindsey's fingers tightened into a fist at his back, "don't leave any crumbs.

Change the data file, use a different IP." But as the words left his mouth the screen went still.

Cedric craned his neck to look back at Zach and Lindsey. "I'm in," he said. "That was fast. She doesn't even use a two-step verification."

Zach leaned forward and took the mouse, pulling up new screens. "Hold on," he said. "She might not be as dumb as she looks."

"He's right," Lindsey blurted, grabbing the back of the chair. "This is too easy!"

A flash of code appeared in the corner of the screen, a series of red boxes popped then disappeared, and a stream of data surged out. "Shut it down!" Lindsey screamed. "Shut it down now, they're in the network!"

Zach pushed Cedric's chair out of the way and lunged at the back of his system, ripping all of the cords loose from the wall. A spark lit the now darkened wall as the machine's steady whir sputtered and stopped.

"No!" Zach cried, as he ripped the computer from the wall and tore the hard drive from the back. "Wipe everything," he yelled, as he pulled open his desk drawer and removed a drill.

"Zach," Lindsey whispered, reaching out to touch his shoulder. "Zach…"

"No," Zach said shaking off her touch. He held the metal hard drive against the desk with one hand then forced a drill bit into its core. "No…" he repeated as he pulled the bit out and drilled in again.

Lindsey turned toward Cedric who had curled his long hands around the back of his neck, an anguished look darkening his face. When he saw Lindsey, he just shook his head. "It's too late," he whispered.

"No," Zach said, running to the microwave. He put the drive inside and hit start. Within seconds the microwave sputtered, flashed, then shut down, smoke drifting from inside.

Lindsey walked up behind him. "Zach, it's okay, we —"

"It's not okay, Lindsey," Zach said, whipping toward her, his eyes aglow. "It's not. They backtracked us. They used a worm."

"Oh, God," Lindsey swallowed. "Did the worm get all the way back to us? Was the real code still in there? Did they — ?"

Zach nodded. "They got it."

Lindsey's stomach lurched as she saw the pained look in Zach's eyes. "We'll fix it," she said, reaching out for him. "We'll turn them in. They should be prosecuted, right? If we sound the alarm they couldn't possibly get away with actually using the code. Right?" she asked furtively. "Right, Zach?"

A bitter laugh dropped from Zach's lips. "You know how paranoid I am, baby. I only kept one copy...and now she's got it. It's over."

Chapter 26: Zach

"She lied to us," Lindsey whispered, curling her long limbs around him.

Zach stroked the back of her neck with the tips of his fingers. "It's easy to lie to you, Lindsey," he said softly. "You're good. It's hard to lie to me. I'm a cynic."

"No, you're not," she said, placing the palm of her hand flat over his heart. "You're brilliant. Everything will all work out in the end. You'll see."

A baffled smile wandered across his lips as he lay in her arms. *How did she do it?* Lindsey remained positive even when he felt like a building had fallen right on top of him.

"I don't think so, Lindz. God only knows who has our code and what they'll do with it. There's no way to fight it. If we turn them in, the dean will just deny it, and we have no proof. So, we're stuck, and the world as I knew it is over."

Lindsey sat up, her pale shoulders and breasts luminous against the sun-kissed warmth of his own skin. "Well, then, I guess we'll just have to create a new world for you."

"Like what?" Zach laughed.

"Dunno," she answered, her lips curving into half a smile. "What did you like to do when you were a kid?"

"Read code."

"Other than that, silly."

"Alright." Zach sat up next to her, pulling her torso close to his. "I really liked eating breakfast on Sunday mornings and watching cartoons."

"Me too! Bugs Bunny?"

"Bugs was okay, but I was more of a Scooby-doo guy."

"I could see that." She nodded. "What was your favorite cereal?"

"I don't really eat cereal."

"What? Impossible. How do you feel about Rice Crispies?"

"What? No."

"Cocoa Puffs?"

He shook his head and squeezed her closer. "Never tried it."

"Wow, sheltered," she said kissing his shoulder. "Okay, how about the grand-daddy, best sugary kid cereal of all time: Fruity Pebbles."

He laughed. "No, baby, I've never had Fruity

Pebbles, either."

"Never? That's criminal," she said. "At least now I know what to get you for Christmas."

Zach wrapped his arms around her shoulder and dropped his head into a corner of light that was stabbing through the blinds. "It's another day," he said in disbelief.

Lindsey turned to glare at the window, then kissed him gently on the shoulder, sending a tingle along his skin. "You know," she said, "Kate says there's nothing a long walk in the sunshine and a tall glass of water won't fix."

"Kate's never really gone through hell, then."

"Oh, she has," Lindsey said, "she just always finds a way through...to see the good parts."

"Okay," Zach said. "I'll bite. Like what?"

"Like...if this all hadn't happened, we never would have met."

"True, baby," Zach said, running his hand gently up and down her thigh. "And, when I'm fired, the dean can't bust me for dating a student."

"See? There's the spirit!" Lindsey laughed. "Like she has any room to judge."

"I know, right? And, if we hadn't met, I never would have cracked the code. I still feel kind of proud I did that."

"You should."

"You should, too. It's your work that put us over the line. I just figured out how to put the pieces together."

"Really? Ah, thanks."

"I told you, Lindsey. You're amazing. And, at least, you'll get your degree, right? There is so much more in store for you...after this."

"After this? I don't want there to be an after this," she said, her lips pouty. "I want to stay in this room with you forever."

"If only that were possible," he said, tilting her jaw toward his and kissing her tenderly. Her lips lingered against his for a long moment, then she slid her hand over his chest, pushing herself up and over him to straddle his waist. She looked down into his eyes as her hands grazed the smooth skin of his chest and abdomen below her, then she spread her hips wider, leaned in, and kissed him again. The warmth of her body made blood rush to his groin. He slid his hands around her hips and the back of her ass, and was about to drag her onto him fully when she pulled back.

"Wait," she said. "Oh my God."

"What?"

Lindsey put her fingers up to her mouth. "That code wouldn't have been cracked without me?"

Zach frowned. "Right..."

"Am I a hired gun?" she asked, going pale. "Holy crap, I am a hired gun."

"What are you talking about?" Zach said, gripping her hips so they remained still.

"For the dean!" she said, closing her eyes. "Maybe we didn't mean to, but if I hadn't helped, she wouldn't have the code." Her eyes shot open. "We have to fix it."

He gripped her thighs and shook his head. "There is no we."

Lindsey's face dropped. "What? What do you mean there's no *we*?"

"I mean, it's my problem," he said. "I'm responsible. Not you."

Lindsey grimaced. "You can't do that to me."

"Do what to you?"

"I can't earn my degree for something so awful. We created this problem together," she said. "We should handle it together."

He shook his head against the pillow. "Nope. No way. You need to go and do great things after this. I can't...if I jammed you up I'd never forgive myself."

"Now you know how I feel," Lindsey said, crossing her arms over her bare chest. "I don't want *you* to be jammed up." Zach didn't reply, and as the moment went by, Lindsey's cheeks went pale. "Do you not trust me?" she whispered. "Still?"

Zach felt his heart clench. "No, I do trust you. I do."

"Then let me help. We can figure it out," she said, laying her hands gently against his chest.

Her eyes waited, wide and hopeful as they searched his face. "Alright, Lindsey. But no jeopardizing your future. Deal?"

"Deal!" She grinned. "So, what do we do now?

Think..."

Zach ran his hands through his hair then lifted her up and over to the other side of the bed. "Alright, well, I can't think with you on top of me." He grinned, lifting her off.

"Fair enough." She smiled, covering herself with the sheet and crossing her legs. "The sooner we get the code back, the sooner we can lay in bed for days. Do you think Blackburton already has it?"

Zach released a long breath. "Maybe."

"Then let's hack Blackburton."

"We couldn't do it fast enough. Plus, we don't even know if they have it or where it's stored."

"What if we just talked to the dean? Maybe she doesn't realize what she's done."

"Oh, she does. She's a predator and we don't have what she—"

"What?" Lindsey asked, her eyes wide. "What is it?"

His mind spun. "She never takes the first deal. She told me that." He turned to Lindsey. "Maybe she's holding it, waiting for the best offer?"

"So, let's find a new way to hack her and find out!" Lindsey said, curling her limbs beneath her and sitting up.

"No, she's too smart for that. No *way* would it be that easy. If you were surrounded by hackers, would you leave the file where they could get it? It has to be off network."

"I see your point," Lindsey said, slumping back

down. "So we have a hacker's dilemma: what do you do when you need a file that is completely off grid?"

"Keep it local," Zach said, drumming his hands on the bed at the thought. "So, where would you keep it?"

Lindsey leaned forward and grabbed Zach by both shoulders, her eyes bright. "I have no idea," she said, a grin spreading across her face. "But we know who might…"

Zach shot upright. "James."

"Right," Lindsey said. "And he doesn't know we're after him."

Chapter 27: Lindsey

"You two live on top of each other?" Cedric asked, looking out the window and down to the sidewalk below. "That must be convenient."

"Oh, the jokes never stop," Zach said flatly.

"Let me have my fun, it helps me relax," Cedric turned, revealing a t-shirt that read, 'I love toxic waste'. "Is he ever going to get here?"

Lindsey ungripped her phone to glare at the screen again. "Last text said he was on his way. Maybe he won't show?"

"Oh no, honey," Cedric said. "Not if he thinks a booty call is going down. He'll crawl here on his hands and knees if he has to."

"I guess," Lindsey shrugged. "Oh! It's him," she said as her phone pinged. "He's parking."

Zach turned toward Cedric. "You ready?"

"I've never been so excited in all my life. But I

still don't know why you wouldn't let me dress like a cop."

"I hope that's a yes," Zach said, turning toward Lindsey. "You get the door, then leave it to us."

Lindsey nodded and joined Cedric at the window. Her pulse raced as she saw James round the corner on the sidewalk below the building. He tucked a six pack under his arm and popped up his collar. "I don't even like beer," she mumbled.

"I'm sure it's for him," Zach said, walking up beside them and looking outside.

"Probably," Lindsey said, her voice quivering.

Zach turned and looked at her, his eyes steady. "It's all going to work out," he said, putting his strong arms around her. Lindsey nodded into his shoulder, taking in the woody clean scent of his skin. As he gave her a final deep squeeze, she could feel the warmth of his skin pulsing through his sweater.

Zach pulled away and jerked his head toward Cedric. As the two walked toward her bedroom, Zach threw Lindsey a wink then ducked inside behind Cedric and closed the door.

Lindsey ran her hands down her jeans and looked at her front door. A knock came, sounding like the top of a bottle was tapping against the wood. With a final glance toward the closed bedroom, Lindsey opened the door.

James leaned against the door jam, a practiced look of boredom playing on his face. "Hey," he said, jerking his head in an upward nod. "I'm here."

"Yup," Lindsey said, pulling the door open. "Lucky me."

James breezed past her, the stench of booze trailing behind him. "Cute place," he said, popping open his beer and taking a drink. "Want one?"

Lindsey shook her head. "Nope. Too early for me."

"What?" he said, his arms wide. "It's the end of the semester. Party time."

"Sit down, James," she said, motioning toward the sofa.

"Ooh, why?" James said, grinning and taking a seat. "Are naughty things going to happen to me here?"

"No," Zach said, coming out of the bedroom. "But naughty things are going to happen if you don't listen."

As Cedric walked out behind Zach, James jerked his head from Cedric to Zach and back to Lindsey. Lindsey gave him a coy smile then locked the bolt on the front door with a decisive pop. James darted off the sofa, beer splashing across his shirt. "What the hell?"

"Sit down, pumpkin," Cedric said, putting his fists on each hip like a super-hero. "The professor has something to say."

Zach pulled a chair from Lindsey's kitchen table and pulled it directly across from James. "Sit down," he said quietly, glaring at James with unflinching eyes. James sank back into the sofa and tried to lean back, casually crossing his legs. "What's up?" he asked.

Zach straddled the back of the wooden chair and leaned forward, his light eyes drilling a hole into James. "Are you familiar with U.S.C. 1029, James?" he asked.

James' mouth dropped open an inch as a tepid laugh sputtered loose. "What is this? Did my frat put you up to this?"

"U.S.C. 1029," blurted Cedric. "The professor asked you a question, sparky."

"Screw you, Cedric," James muttered.

"Lovely," Cedric said. "I guess that's that. I told you. He's too dumb to help himself."

James whipped his head around toward Lindsey. "What the hell? You invited me here for this bullshit?"

"You'd better listen, James," she said, almost feeling bad for him. "If you haven't guessed, you're in some trouble here."

Zach continued. "1029 is a federal law against the creation and distribution of codes that give hackers unauthorized access to computer systems. That's federal, meaning federal prison time."

Lindsey watched as James' face faded from red to white. "I didn't...what?"

"And," Zach continued, "U.S.C. 1030 is another federal law which forbids access to government computers. I could go on."

James shook his head, closing his eyes for a moment. "I don't know what this is, but I haven't hacked into any government systems."

"We know that," Zach said. "But the Feds won't. They'll only see the trail of code we'll upload if you don't cooperate."

James turned again toward Lindsey, his face slack. "But I—" He shook his head. "What are they saying?"

"What we're saying," Cedric said, "is things are going to get pretty rough if you don't finally get that self-righteous stick out of your ass."

"James," Zach said, holding up a hand, silencing Cedric. "We don't want to hurt you. Really. But we know what you did with the dean."

A car honked from the street below as James blinked and assessed his situation. He reached up and ran his hand down his beer stained chest before speaking. "She made me," he said, curling his arms around his waist. "She was so aggressive. It was totally gross."

"For God's sake, not *that*," Zach said, wiping his brow roughly. "You installed a worm in her system."

James blinked rapidly. "Yeah, so?"

Zach pulled his chair closer and leaned in. "So, she back-doored us. She stole the code."

James looked at him blankly. "So."

Zach lunged at James, his chair flipping beneath him. "Dammit, James! You know what that code can do!"

Lindsey rushed over and put a calming hand on Zach. As her fingertips ran down the muscles of his back, she could feel his heart pounding. She took her other hand and put it on his forearm, holding him there until his breathing slowed.

After a moment, she picked up the chair with her fingertips and sat down next to James. "You have a plan, right?" she asked, trying to divert his panicked eyes in her direction. "After graduation? I looked at your algorithm," she said. "It's good."

James blinked, then tried to swallow, his adams-apple bobbing in his throat. "Really?"

"Yeah, you can always sell it to someone else."

"I tried," he practically sobbed. "Graduation is almost here and no one was interested. The dean promised she had a buyer. I didn't think…I—"

Cedric stepped forward. "I have a question. Did you at least get paid? Was it worth stabbing us all in the back to sell your silly equation?"

James didn't need to respond. The sob that bubbled up his throat was response enough.

"Of course, not. Rookie," Cedric blurted.

Lindsey gave James a calming look. "It's okay," she said. "What good is a stack of cash if the world goes to hell, anyway, right?"

James shrugged. "Philanthropy. You can't help people until you have money, Lindsey."

"Not true," she said, reaching out for his hand. "You can help right now. It's not too late."

A boozy hiccup escaped from James as he looked at Lindsey. "How?"

"You set up her systems, right? Does she keep one at her house?

James nodded. "In the den. But you can't hack in, it's offline."

"Let us handle that," quipped Zach, his arms crossed near the window.

"What about my algorithm," he asked, his eyes flooding. "Can you get that back too?"

Lindsey jumped as several knocks hit the door. "They're here."

Zach looked at his watch. "Bedroom," he said, "keep them out of here."

Lindsey nodded then opened the front door.

"Hey, Lindsey," Heather said, sweeping into the room carrying several garment bags, followed by Brie and Taylor. "I thought you'd never call us."

"Sorry, been busy."

Heather looked over the scene in the living room. "I guess," she said, her eyes darting from face to face. "Hey, Professor Wheeler," she smiled.

"Let's go in the bedroom," Lindsey said quickly.

"Oh," Brie said, fluffing her hair. "James is here too. Hey, James."

James swallowed. "Hey."

Lindsey walked to her bedroom door and opened it. "In here," she said. As the three girls followed her inside, she gave Zach a nod, then shut the door.

"Professor Wheeler, huh?" Heather whispered to Lindsey, unzipping the top of a garment bag. "You *are* a smart bitch."

"He's just my professor," Lindsey said, wishing she could still hear the conversation in the living room.

"Whatevs. Your secret's safe with us. You are going to love this one," Heather said, pulling out a white dress. "It's one of mine."

"I brought one, too!" Brie said, holding up another garment. "And so did Taylor."

Heather exhaled loudly. "The point is, you get to choose. What is this swank party you're going to anyway?"

Lindsey walked over to the bed and ran her fingers down the fabric of the white dress. "Winter Party at the dean's house."

"Dean Cruz?" Heather said. "*Gaudy.*"

"Shameless," Brie said.

Taylor shrugged. "She's okay."

"She could take advice from us, that's for sure." Heather said. "Do you see how much jewelry she wears? Like Coco Channel said, 'always remove a piece before leaving the house'."

"Edit," Brie nodded.

Lindsey could barely take in what they were saying. She was focused on the voices rising outside the bedroom door.

Chapter 28: Zach

Zach felt the air leave his body the moment she opened the door. Lindsey glowed, her pale skin shining against the red silk of her dress. His brain dropped all the thoughts that had been swirling within; nothing remaining but the sudden strong beat of his own heart.

"Hi," she said, her lips red and soft as rose petals. "Well...what do you think?"

"God, Lindsey, you look so fucking good."

A smile played at her lips. She turned once so he could see the back of her dress, and the black seam that ran up the back of her stockings. As she swung back around, she stopped and looked wide-eyed at Zach. "What...?"

Zach swallowed, then lunged forward, his blood thick in his ears. Before she could say another word, his mouth was on hers. She tensed for a moment, then loosened and curled her arms around him, giving into the sudden force of his desire. As his mouth dropped to the nape of her neck, he heard her take a breath, rough and deep, the sound making him grow thicker, straining against the fabric of his pants.

Her small breasts tilted upwards with the arch of her back, cupped perfectly by the cut of her dress. He pulled one hand away from her and ran it along the material so fine he could feel the curve of her torso beneath his fingers. He traced her belly back up to the top of the fabric, lingering at the edge of the bodice, every muscle in his arm longing to rip it off of her body.

"Zach," she whispered, "I…"

"You what?" he asked, feeling her heat rise against him.

"I…I wish we had more time."

Zach's mind raced back to center as he pulled away. Her lipstick was smeared across her chin, matching the red that flushed her cheeks.

"Right." He smiled, raising his hand up to his mouth.

"Yeah." Lindsey grinned. "It's all over you, too." She led him to the bathroom where they washed the lipstick from their faces. She pulled out a tube and began to re-apply the color, her lips parted slightly, her pink tongue behind her teeth within. Zach wondered how he would ever keep his eyes off of her at the party. "You're beautiful," he said.

Lindsey turned her almond eyes toward him and let out a long, slow breath. "You are, too." she said, taking a final look in the mirror before speaking to Zach's reflection. "Hey, what was all that stuff about the U.S.C laws?"

Zach shrugged. "I wasn't always so straight. As a kid, I hacked into the base where we were stationed. My dad had to take early retirement."

"Wow."

"Don't look so surprised. Cedric wasn't the only hacker my brother saved."

"Hello?" A voice came from the living room.

Zach and Lindsey emerged from the bathroom to see Cedric clad in a waiter's uniform, his face free of makeup.

"Don't look that surprised," Cedric said. "We can't all go in all dolled up like supermodels. One of us should be invisible, and believe me, waiters are invisible. I learned that early, which is why I settled on a life of crime."

"Cedric—" Zach began.

"Alright, Professor, I just say that to poke at you. I'm on the straight and narrow now."

"You look...nice." Lindsey said.

"Nice? Just kick me in the balls why don't you," Cedric said, pulling out a box with three tiny earpieces. "In addition to this heinous outfit, I procured a catering van."

"Cedric..." Zach said again.

"Relax. I didn't steal it. I have friends," Cedric said, handing Zach one of the earpieces then a USB. "As planned, you find her system and pop in this VPN. From the van, I'll remote in and steal our baby back."

"Speaking of friends," Lindsey said, "what happened with James?"

"We came to an understanding. He gave me her password. *SexyJ6969.*" Zach said, fitting in his ear piece. "Can you see it?" he asked Lindsey, bending down.

"No," Lindsey said, putting in her own ear piece. "How about me?"

"You're good," Zach answered. "I'm sure James had to change his underwear when he got home, but I think he learned a good lesson today."

"Yeah, bless his little heart," Cedric added, turning on his microphone. "We sent him away to cry in his six-pack and contemplate his new reality. Testing," he said into it. "Testing, can you hear me alright?"

Zach and Lindsey nodded.

"Unfortunately," Cedric continued, "I can't hear you guys, but at least I can tell you when it's done." Zach and Lindsey nodded again. "Alright then," Cedric continued. "After we get the program, assuming we get the program, load the file attached to the USB. Her system will never recover."

"Got it," Zach said.

"And I'll be a lookout," Lindsey said. "No one

will get near you while you're in there."

Zach frowned. "We talked about this. You promised you wouldn't jeopardize yourself."

"Oh, I see, Professor," Cedric said. "It's okay if we get caught, just not Miss Lindsey here."

"No one is getting caught," Lindsey said, grabbing them both by the hand. "This is going to work."

"Alright," Cedric sang, "That's the spirit. Now hold on to your nuts and nips, people, we are going to rob the dean."

Chapter 29: Lindsey

They pulled up the circular drive behind three other cars and idled in silence as valets leaped to open the car doors ahead of them. Lindsey turned and peered nervously at the line of cars rolling up behind them. Her fingers gripped the handle of the door as she waited their turn, feeling suddenly trapped.

"You good?" Zach asked, placing his hand on hers.

She exhaled at the sound of his voice. "Yeah," she answered. "I'm ready."

His light eyes shone in the dim winter sun. "Not too late to turn back."

"What? And miss all the fun?" she said, grinning. "No way."

An engine revved behind them, a signal to pull forward. Zach put the car in gear and they moved ahead to a waiting valet in a red vest. "Okay," he said as another valet pulled open Lindsey's door. "Let's do this."

Lindsey stepped out next to the browning front lawn of the dean's house and waited for Zach to circle around the car. A light melody could be heard from the sweeping veranda overlooking the property, the happy rhythms making her feel suddenly disjointed and out of place. She grabbed for Zach's hand as he reached her and gripped it tightly as they began to walk forward, up the meandering sidewalk ahead. Zach switched hands so he could put the palm of his massive hand reassuringly on the small of her back. Together, they ascended the holiday adorned front steps and walked through the front door.

The cool outside air gave way to stifling humidity as a swarm of people enveloped them in the foyer. Even in heels and taller than most, Lindsey wished she could see over all the heads and get a lay of the house. She had no idea where they were going. Zach must, because he steered her silently through the crowd, past a coat-check, then a bar, and suddenly into an adjacent hallway. She felt the warm skin of his arms wrap around her. "How am I going to do this?" he whispered. "I can't take my eyes off of you."

Lindsey tilted her head up toward his jaw and smiled. "You have to. Otherwise the plan won't work."

"I—," he began, shaking his head. "I mean, I don't want to leave you. What if something happens? What if we get caught?"

Lindsey wrapped her hand under his open jacket and around the taut muscles of his lower back. "Nothing's going to happen."

"If you don't graduate, I'll never forgive myself," he said.

Her other hand reached up to his chest, feeling the thumping of his heart. "Let's save the world," she said, softly. "*Then* I'll graduate. It's going to be okay," Lindsey said. "You'll see."

Zach squeezed his eyes shut, took a breath then looked at her. "Okay," he said, giving her a final squeeze. "See you on the flip side."

As Lindsey watched Zach's large frame squeeze back through the crowd, she tried to remember the schematic of the house and gain her bearings. The den was adjacent to the Great Room, which she believed was around the corner. She stepped away from the hall and squared her shoulders, hoping she hadn't gotten turned around. As she did, a waiter approached with a tray of champagne. "Why don't you take two, lovely," he said.

Lindsey looked up to see Cedric before her. "One is fine," she said, lifting a glass from the tray.

"This is so exciting!" Cedric said like a ventriloquist through clenched teeth, then peeled away and made his way out the front door. Lindsey stepped to a large adjoining window and watched

Cedric ditch his tray, dodge a crowd to get past the sidewalk, then around a hedge to step into the side of a white van. There was a sting of static in her ear, then she heard Cedric's voice. "The crow flies at midnight, over," he said. "I repeat, the crow flies at midnight."

Lindsey sipped at her bubbles and wished she could say something back. Instead, she scowled out the window.

"I always wanted to say that," Cedric said into her ear. "Alright, party-people, we are live. I am ready for espionage to ensue. Over."

Lindsey downed her glass and took a right into the Great Room. Through a mass of faces, she saw Zach at the top of a row of stairs. As if she had called his name, he turned and met her eye. Lindsey swept forward knowing he was watching her, and found an empty chair near the hallway to the den. She feigned a casual lean against it then turned back toward Zach. He gave her an almost imperceptible nod, began to move toward the den, but was abruptly thwarted by the dean.

Lindsey gasped and moved slightly to her right, hoping to see the look on Zach's face. She couldn't be sure, but she thought he was smiling. He was speaking, and the dean nodded. She wished again Cedric had gotten their microphones to work so she could hear what they were saying. Lindsey put down her glass and took a step to her right, but then, she too, was blocked.

"Did you mean what you said?"

Lindsey looked up to see James, his jaw slack and reeking of booze. "Not now, James," she said, pivoting left.

"Wait," he slurred. "Wait, you said I could do good."

"Go away," she demanded, practically hissing. "You're drunk."

"I know, I know, I know. Redundant much?" he mumbled to himself, then laughed. "Seriously, listen. I know you guys all hate me."

"We don't. But right now," she said, looking over his shoulder, "you need to go away."

"I want to do good, Lindsey," he said, dragging her name out.

"Okay, you do that. Now go."

He teetered slightly. "Okey dokey, Lindsey-Pinsey."

Lindsey bent to her right. Zach was still trapped by the dean, except now he was frowning. "Damn it, James!" she said, pushing him to the side.

James leaned back and squinted, trying to get a clear view of Lindsey's face. "What? What do you keep looking at?" he said, turning. "Oh," he said. "Dean is cock-blocking the Prof. Crash and burn."

"I don't know what you're talking about," Lindsey said. "Go. Away."

James reached his hand up to his swollen face and breathed into his palm, trying to get a sense of his breath. "I got this," he said, spinning around about fifteen degrees too far. He corrected himself, then began to walk directly toward the dean.

Lindsey's arm sprung out, trying to catch James by the back of his jacket, but it was too late. As his blond hair bobbed through the crowd, Lindsey waved her arms in Zach's direction. He said something to the dean, his words animated by the scowl on his face, then he turned and saw her.

She pointed at James coming his way. His eyes flew from James to the dean, and back to Lindsey. Lindsey pointed toward the den then gestured with her hands that she needed five minutes.

Zach shook his head perceptibly and mouthed the word, "No."

Lindsey watched his brow strain as he stared at her, his eyes begging her not to go. She spoke back into the abyss. "I love you," she said, blew him a kiss, and walked out of sight.

Chapter 30: Zach

"What are you doing here, Professor Wheeler?" The dean asked. "Just couldn't stay away from me, could you?"

Zach tore his eyes from Lindsey and forced himself to wield the most natural smile he could. "I wouldn't miss your famous Winter Party, Dean."

"Really," she sang, her thick makeup competing with the jewelry dangling from her neck and arms. "That's a surprise."

"How so?" Zach asked, as Lindsey stared from across the room.

"You hate these functions. Besides, we both know my invitation was really a…formality."

Zach shook his head. "What? I wouldn't miss the celebration. Especially now that our project is done."

Dean Cruz gave a small laugh and raised her

glass. "Yes," she said. "The project. Aren't you adorable?"

Zach flinched. "How so?"

"You're a terrible liar. Let me tell you why you're really here. You know I have the real code and you want it back."

His heart lurched. "Real code? I don't follow—"

"Stop. Honestly, it's so unattractive."

"Fine," Zach seethed. "You have it. But I'm sure, if you knew what that program could do in the wrong hands, you wouldn't sell it. Right?"

"Sell it?" Her mouth curved. "Why, I would only do that with the permission of the university. After all, your work-product is, and always will be, property of this university."

Zach took her in, the black of her eyeliner sliding into the corner of her eyes, making her look more snake-like than ever. "I didn't know Blackburton was in the market for university property."

The dean's smile fell into a crooked line. "This university, and your position, are both funded by my efforts. Remember that."

Zach felt a black pit swell in his stomach—this was a mistake. He glanced over to Lindsey, hoping to give her a signal to run when he saw her long arms waving above the crowd. She pointed feverishly into the pack of faces below, through which James was approaching. His eyes shot back to Lindsey. She pointed at her wrist, blew Zach a kiss, and disappeared down the hall toward the den. His heart lurched. It was too late to stop her.

"You can say *no* all you want," the dean said, "but the fact is, I run this place. Get on board, or get out."

Before Zach could respond, James plowed through and fell against him. "What is this?" he yelled at the dean, swaying. "You want *him*, now?"

Dean Cruz leaned back, her eyes pivoting to take in all the heads that were turning their way. "Have you lost your mind?" She spat.

James lunged forward and grabbed her around the waist, forcing his mouth onto hers. "You're mine!" he yelled, pulling back, and throwing a wink at Zach. "Play along," he mouthed to Zach silently. "Leave my girl alone!"

Zach put up his hands with a look of shocked surrender.

The dean wiped her mouth. "Stop it. You imbecile." She hissed at James. "People are—wait," she asked, her eyes wide. "Do you think I'm an idiot?" She swung toward Zach. "Did you really think this would work? Where is your star student right now?"

"I really don't know what you mean," Zach said. "Perhaps, your own indiscretions are coming back to bite you."

Her eyes shot open, then narrowed into a sneer. She pivoted to her right, then shot through the crowd and toward a security guard. Zach ran after her, his blood running cold as he heard her words. "Officer Jones," she said as the guard approached. "There is a thief in my house."

Zach looked at Jones, giving him a tiny shake of his head, just as James ran up behind him, coughing and short of breath.

Officer Jones hooked his thumbs into his belt and took in their faces. "I'm a bit confused, Dean."

The dean scowled. "I'll speak more slowly, then. There is a thief in this house. A student. She's here to rob me."

"Alright, Ma'am," Officer Jones said. "I can look around. But, what exactly should I be looking for?"

Zach's blood ran cold. If they found Lindsey in the dean's den, they would all go to jail. "Nobody's stealing from you, Dean," he said. "I just came to talk to you." He glanced at the growing pack of onlookers and lowered his voice. "I'm sure we can work this out," he said. "Privately."

The dean tapped her pointy fingertips across her necklace as she considered his words. "Perhaps, Professor —," she began.

"Thief!" James bellowed. "Exactly! There she is!" he said, pointing at Dean Cruz.

"Shut up!" she yelled.

Zach felt his breath stop. Anger washed across the dean's face. All compassion had been purged from her eyes.

"What is going on here?" President Sanders asked, teetering up on his cane. "Why is everyone screaming?"

Zach turned to President Sanders. "President," he said, hoping he could distract everyone long enough to give Lindsey the time she needed. "I believe Dean Cruz is attempting to steal university property."

The president's bushy, white eyebrows rose high as his eyes widened. "That's a serious charge, Professor."

"It's true!" James broke in. "It's on her computer. I can show you!"

Zach felt all the blood drain from his face. "No," he said. "No... *shut up*, James."

The president's white eyebrows rose in shock. "What on earth is going on here, Dean? Is this some kind of joke?"

The dean stepped toward Zach, her words cutting through the mumbles of the onlookers. "So, she's in my office, huh?" she sneered, then turned toward the president. "No joke, I'm afraid. Professor Wheeler's new star is attempting a burglary as we speak. When we find her, she will be expelled and prosecuted. Jones," she said. "You're with me!"

Chapter 31: Lindsey

Lindsey closed the door to the den quietly behind her and sat at the dean's computer. She swiped the mouse across the desk and the monitor lit up, revealing a screen saver littered with pictures of cut diamonds. She perched her trembling fingers above the keyboard and began to type as fast as she could. Her fingers flew to ctrl/alt/delete in an effort to over-ride the system. A box popped up: USER ID: SYSTEM. Lindsey typed in the password: Sexy*J6969*, then hit enter.

The system responded, Invalid authorization code: access denied.

"Crap, crap, crap," Lindsey muttered.

She tried again. USER ID: SYSTEM. Password: Sexy*J6969*.

As she hit enter, the desktop opened up. "Thank, God," she said. Immediately, her mouse flew down to examine the network. James was right —the dean's system wasn't connected to the internet. No wires in, no wires out. Her heart lurched; the VPN they needed to send the code out to the van was still in Zach's pocket.

"Think, Lindsey, think, think, think," she muttered to herself. Her eyes flew around the room. She didn't even see a printer. She slid open the desk drawer slowly, hoping the creaking noise didn't arouse suspicion from people walking up and down the hallway outside. Her hands rifled through pens, loose keys, condoms, and what looked like a silver pack of cards. Lindsey grabbed it. "Yes," she squealed as she plugged it into the side of the terminal. Dozens of file folders popped up, but none were the team's master code.

"You dirty mother," Lindsey muttered as her eyes took in an avalanche of skin. There were dozens of revealing photos, all of male students in compromising positions. Attached to each picture was a series of documents, mostly recommendations the dean had given. In the upper right corner, she saw James' face staring back at her. She clicked on his picture, trying not to look at what was exposed and instead clicked on the attached document. His algorithm lit up the screen. Hearing voices trailing down the hall, she cut his algorithm and erased it from the drive. At least she could do that. Now, if she could only find their master code, she could load it on this external hard drive and get back out to Zach.

A whine shot through her ear piece. "What is going on in there?" she heard Cedric say. "Professor? Is everything alright?"

Lindsey silenced her ear piece, concentrating on her fingers and her new search of the computer's hard drive. She searched in every corner for their program, but each time the same answer popped up. Search results: 0. Lindsey gripped the edges of the keyboard. The file wasn't there and voices in the hall were getting louder. She and Zach would have to come up with a new plan. She quickly erased her trail and put the computer back to sleep. She pushed away from the desk with the hard drive still in her hand and sprinted across the den toward the door. Her hand flew up to push the door open, right as someone pulled it from the other side. Instead of pushing on wood, Lindsey's fingers pushed right into the stiff face of Dean Cruz.

"Oh!" Lindsey cried as she fell into the hallway, the hard drive flying out into a sea of feet. "Sorry."

The dean stepped back and tried to smooth the invisible mark of Lindsey's fingers away from her cheeks. "Ms. Monahan, I assume."

Lindsey looked up at the range of faces squeezed into the hallway, including Zach's, which looked stunned and completely drained of blood. Beside him stood President Sanders, a teetering James, and Officer Jones. As Zach reached out and helped Lindsey up, she kicked the hard drive out of sight.

"President Sanders," the dean announced, "this student, at the behest of her professor, was just attempting to steal my personal property."

"What?" Lindsey said, holding up her empty hands. "Sorry, I didn't know this area was off limits. I was just looking for the bathroom."

The dean stepped forward, pushing her chest just inches from Lindsey. "You are expelled. Officer, Jones," she continued, "escort Ms. Monahan from this property."

Lindsey's jaw dropped open. She wanted to say something but her mouth was dry. Zach pushed forward. "What proof do you have?" he asked the dean. "You can't accuse people without proof."

"Yes, Dean Cruz," President Sanders said. "It goes both ways. We can't expel a student without evidence she has violated the code of ethics."

"I know Lindsey," Officer Jones broke in. "I don't believe she — ."

"James!" The dean called over the voices. "Go to my computer. Pull up the activity log."

James exhaled loudly through slack lips. "I don't work for you anymore, lady." he sputtered. "I'm with the professor, now."

"Enough!" President Sanders said. "Professor Wheeler, explain yourself. What is going on here?"

Zach stepped forward and stood next to Lindsey, silently touching the very tip of her shoe with his own. She looked up and saw the question in his eyes. With a little shake of her head, she told him: *we didn't get it.*

Zach dropped his head then put his hand on the small of Lindsey's back. "President Sanders," he said, raising his eyes. "The dean has been stealing our work and plotting to sell it to a third party."

"Absurd!" The dean said indignantly. "That's slander. Your career is over, Wheeler."

Lindsey leaned against Zach, wanting to absorb some of the pain she knew he was feeling. She remembered his tender words, that when you care about someone, you want to keep them close. She felt the same. In a rush, the words took on new meaning. The things you care about you want to keep close! Her head spun as her eyes washed over the dean. As she did, her heart began to pump with blood. Over the heads of the growing crowd, she saw a drink tray plowing through. It was Cedric. As their eyes met, she began to beat her hand against her chest and cast her eyes toward the dean. Cedric gasped, then nodded.

"Excuse me," he said, pushing his way forward. "Thank you, excuse me, drinks to serve." Just behind the dean, he tripped, the drinks cascading forward along with the tray. Cedric slammed against the dean, who slammed into the wall and collapsed to the floor.

"Oh my God, Ma'am," Cedric said, pulling her up by the arm. "I am so, so sorry." He flipped a white cloth out of his back pocket and ran it over her dress, trying to erase the dewy specks of liquid that had cascaded across it. Then he bent down on one knee to pick up a broken glass, and ran the white cloth over the hard drive, making it disappear.

"Out! Out!" screamed the dean. "All of you, out of my house!"

The president pushed forward on his cane. "Stop," he said.

The dean turned, her hair falling over one black smudged eye. "What?" she snapped.

"The professor has leveled a serious accusation against you," he said. "What is your response?"

The dean scoffed. "My response? It's ludicrous! My response is that I want his tenure stripped. He is a failure and a loon."

The president turned to Zach, a grave look on his face. "Do you have evidence?" he asked again.

Zach shook his head.

Lindsey grabbed him by the arm. "We do now," she whispered.

Zach's head whipped toward her. "We do?"

Lindsey nodded, pointing toward the dean. Zach turned, and saw the large pendant that hung from the dean's neck was now gone, a thin silver string hanging loosely in its place. Lindsey watched as relief swept through Zach's body. "We do." He grinned, turning toward President Sanders. "We do have evidence. She stole our code to sell to a defense contractor. We can prove it."

Dean Cruz lunged forward and teetered off her high heel. "Out! Out!" she cried, grabbing Officer Jones by the elbow and pushing him forward. "I want them all out."

President Sanders shook his head. "No, Dean. This house is university property. I am instructing Officer Jones to escort you out until a full investigation can be waged.

Officer Jones exhaled and threw Zach and Lindsey a smile. "Happy to," he said. "Ma'am?" Dean Cruz spun on her remaining shoe and began to hyperventilate. "Don't you touch me!" she screamed at Jones, her arms swinging in the air.

Onlookers began to fall back quietly, gathering their coats and mumbling in stunned voices as they walked toward their cars. Lindsey and Zach followed them, their hands gripped tightly together. They found Cedric leaning against a pillar on the front porch, smoking an electronic cigarette, his waiter uniform draped over a nearby chair.

"Hi, all," he smiled. "Voila!" Against the dark of his skin shone the jewel encrusted pendant, pulled apart to reveal a USB.

"It's all on there?" Zach asked.

"It is," Cedric sang.

A rush of delight enveloped Lindsey and she flew forward, wrapping her arms around Cedric. "Thank goodness for you," she said.

He grinned. "Ah, shucks, I am finally appreciated in my own time."

Zach grabbed Cedric roughly and pulled him into a hug. "Thank you," he said, then turned toward Lindsey. He looked down at her, his face filled with a joy. She reached up and trailed her fingers along his cheek. "We won," she said. "I want to see you this happy forever."

Zach swept her up in his arms and dipped her slightly. "You do?" he said. "Then I won," he said, grinning. "And you'll graduate. Now everyone will want to work with you."

"I guess."

"You guess? Do you still not know how amazing you are?"

"I do, but, what if I want to keep working with you?"

"I'd be lucky, but...I don't want to hold you back."

"I don't want you to hold me back," Lindsey said, wrapping her arms around him. "I just want you to hold me. And never let go."

Epilogue

Lindsey's body lay slack against the pillows, her arm draped over Zach's belly. Every muscle in her body vibrated with a low heat she had never felt before. A distant throbbing beat between her legs and she knew later she would be sore, but didn't care. His fingertips slid along her forearm until her whole body ached to respond. Every move of his hand sent ripples through her torso. She turned, throwing one long leg over him.

"How long can we stay in here?" she asked, her hand moving to the taut skin of his chest.

"Forever," he responded, grinning.

"Won't we need food? Water?"

"Eventually," he responded, leaning over to trail soft kisses from her ear lobe and down the side of her neck.

Lindsey gasped and vaulted herself on top of

him, needing her most tender skin to press fully against him. She felt him respond beneath her. "We can order in," she teased, moving slowly back and forth.

"Uh-huh," he said, shutting his eyes. "Delivery is good."

Lindsey reached forward and touched his bottom lip, which had parted slightly. His skin glowed in the soft light pouring through the windows. She bent forward and laid her mouth on his, touching his lip with the tip of her tongue. As she did, a tiny ping came from the bedside table. Zach grunted as she bent to see the screen.

"It's Kate," she said, pulling a robe over her shoulders. "It's about the funding."

"Okay," Zach said, grabbing her by the hips, "but after this, you're mine."

Lindsey grinned and accepted the call, pulling the phone up to her face. Kate illuminated the screen.

"Hey, Lindz," she called out. "How's everything? How's Zach?"

Lindsey grinned into the screen, pushing herself down against Zach's still swollen groin. "He's great. I don't have long to chat."

"Gotcha," Kate replied. "Did you get the latest email?"

"Yes! You saved us," Lindsey said. "Who knew so many Boston elite would want to see our program go forward?"

"It took ten minutes. I just flipped through my contacts."

"Well, we appreciate it."

"We?" Kate prodded. "Us?"

Lindsey grinned into the phone then down at Zach's beautiful face, smiling back at her. "We're in love. Exhausted, starving, sleep deprived, but totally, utterly in love."

"That's amazing, Lindz!"

"Yeah," Lindsey said, looking back at Kate. "After graduation, we're going to Bora Bora."

"You're kidding me."

"Nope. We got a bungalow over the water for two whole weeks. No computer. No phones. No internet."

"Whose idea was that?"

"His, believe it or not! He wants to take a break before the new semester starts. I'm teaching undergrad, and we're rolling out the new partnership. *We* have a lot of big plans."

Kate beamed. "I'm so proud of you."

"Thanks. I never would have done this without you. We have to celebrate. You and Chase have to come to Boston."

"We will. We'll find a time."

Lindsey smiled down at Zach once more. "We were hoping you had time in the spring, actually. I'm hoping you'll be my Maid of Honor."

"What? Oh my God!"

Zach ran his hands up Lindsey's thighs and

grabbed the phone. Turning it toward his face. "Hey, Kate. Sorry, we have to go now." He hit end and threw the phone to the end of the bed. He flung Lindsey onto her back and hovered over her, pressing himself against her. "I love you," he said, and slid inside of her.

About the Author

Josephine Parker has been writing, reading, and loving books for 30 years. She holds a fine-arts degree in Creative Writing from the University of Colorado-Boulder, and has worked as a literary agent, freelance writer, and editor before embarking on her own dream of owning several small businesses and writing books. She splits her time between Denver and Seattle with the love of her life and their very needy cat.

Josephine followed her own American Dream, and now invites readers to join her heroines in fulfilling their dreams and finding true love.

She also loves to interact with readers. You can find her on twitter **@JosiePBooks**, **facebook.com/josiepbooks** or keep up to date on new releases, free short stories, and her newsletter by going to her website at **jp-books.com.**

She is available for interviews, podcasts, and book clubs.

If you've enjoyed *Loving Lindsey*, please leave a review on the site from which you purchased it. Reviews are the lifeblood of all authors, and I'm no exception! Thank you!

If you haven't read *Chasing Kate ~ Book 1* of the *An American Dream Love Story Series*, you can find it at Amazon.com or other fine retailers!

COMING IN THE FALL OF 2017

Seducing Sienna

An American Dream Love Story
Book 3

Sienna has a secret, and it's not just the recipe she uses in her cupcakes. When cocky U.S. Marshall Sam Wheeler's investigation threatens to expose her, she'll do what she must to shut him out, but can Sienna resist the sweet indulgence he brings?

An American Dream Love Story
Where women chase their dreams and find love

Made in the USA
San Bernardino, CA
07 April 2019